Wish

Deby Adair

I0592546

The Unicorns of Wish Books

(1)

UnicornKisses

Australia

Lovingly dedicated to all the 'four paws'

With sincere love and gratitude to all my 'little unicorns.'
Immeasurably - for Legs - my own faithful Pud.

Cataloguing-in-Publication is held at the National Library of Australia

Adair, Deby
Wish
Revised ed.
ISBN: 978-0-9804513-0-6

Published in Australia 2007
Revised ed. published 2011
Published in USA 2012
Revised ed. published by UnicornKisses 2019

Child and Youth Fiction

The Unicorns of Wish Books
(1)

Cover and Design by UnicornKisses Australia

Join us with other Kindred Spirits
www.unicornkisses.com

Contents

The Legend

Rising from the mists of sunset and reaching into dawn's surprise, there is a land called Wish. Guarded by ponds and watched by noble keepers, Wish awaits and prepares for adventures.

One day, a warrior dressed in splendid clothes, and handsome as he was rich, charged the shores of Wish. His desire was to slay a unicorn. He wanted the golden horn for its hidden powers and wisdom.

No matter how much he was told that a dead unicorn's horn was of no use to anyone, he would not listen and would not be told. He wasn't wanted in Wish and was heartily ignored, but the warrior returned again and again; he would not be swayed. It was his wish and his desire to have the horn of a unicorn. He promised a huge reward to those in the land.

But what did they care for bullion or gold? Would it make them strong? Give them wisdom? Teach them to be brave, kind, or fair?

There lived a sorcerer in Wish, and he too ignored the warrior's plea, but then one sad and foreboding night the sorcerer came forward with a changed mind. And so it was. The sorcerer told the warrior where he could find a unicorn and having done his duty he asked to have his gold, but the warrior was well studied and he knew the ancient lore… mighty unicorns would not appear for just anyone, so he ordered the sorcerer to bring a unicorn to him.

The sorcerer could have taken the gold and sent the warrior home; instead, using wild magic, he changed his appearance and shape to become the image of an innocent maiden.

He sat and waited when all his trickery was complete, on a boulder of a path well used. He held his breath and waited for a sacred unicorn. Meanwhile the warrior hid in bushes nearby, with his arrows and crossbow held ready, his handsome face excited and aglow!

Soon it happened. The wait was neither long nor hard before a pure white unicorn, with shy, soft steps, made herself known. Her breathtaking golden horn shone brightly as her gossamer mane and tail flowed in all their glory to the ground. With innocent eyes open and wide, the unicorn spoke like this: 'With your once kind heart now turned cold, would you sell your soul and kill virtue, for gold? You are not a maiden, so I offer you a chance: withdraw, send the warrior away and save yourself while you can.'

Discovered in his deception, the sorcerer was not humbled. He did not bow his head or beg forgiveness. Furiously he cast away his disguise, and with a twisted face, he cried out to the warrior.

Triumphant, the warrior shot the arrow from his bow with an aim that would surely make its mark, but the unicorn swiftly turned, so her shoulder was pierced and not her heart. She screamed, though, and to hear a unicorn scream is to hear the end of all that is fair.

The sound of her torment was heart-rending, desolate, a thing of dire anguish, and so it was that in that moment, the warrior knew what he had done. With blinding clarity he threw down his arrows and flung away his cruel crossbow, then ran in dread to fall at her feet.

'Forgive me,' he sobbed, 'please forgive my black-hearted soul!'

Although pain throbbed in her sacred horn, and in agony her innocent shoulder bled, the unicorn knew the need for pity and this is what she said: 'Warrior, save yourself while you can. This was your wish, so now, to save your lost soul, you must wish for something to heal my wound.'

The warrior had been unthinking in his deeds; he had craved power and done anything to satisfy the means. Now, with true remorse, he wished to heal her at any price and in the very instant of his wishing he lost his human form to become a small tree with dark green leaves that were trimmed in brightest gold. The unicorn ate several leaves then sure enough, the torn, blood-drenched hole closed over, as if it had never been!

Angered, the sorcerer cursed aloud. He must either run in fear or deal with the living unicorn. With sadness in her velvet eyes, the unicorn turned to him and spoke: 'You are an outcast. You are ugly, damaged, and very, very sad. You have my pity, so I too make a wish and this is what I say: 'Let the gold the warrior paid you, forever disappear. And may you be shunned by all until the day you make amends.'

The riches that the warrior had bestowed vanished, and were never seen again, and so it was that the sorcerer knew defeat, and he cursed with anguish and angry tears.

The unicorn had fulfilled her task. She knew there was nothing left to do, so with the speed of birds and the legs of horse, she galloped away, far away.

For a while, Wish was quiet again.

The Dream's Beginning

Listen carefully, for I know a tale. I heard it from a traveller when I was still a child. Her face was shadowed by a plain brown hood and her cloak rubbed well-worn shoes. Gazing from wonderful, eerie eyes, there strode a dog by her side. They appeared one morning in our village street and, with that instant attraction of something new, like bees drawn to honey, we children ran to their sides as the huge beast let us pat his grey nose.

'Who are you? Who are you?' we boldly called. Then, without hesitation, we took her hands and tugged impatiently at her robe.

'I'm a traveller,' she announced, in such a way that we knew we couldn't let her go. The dog looked up at her as if understanding every word. Smiling at him she murmured, 'And this is my old friend.'

'Where are you from?' we called. 'Where are you going?'

She paused and peered thoughtfully at us, then sat on a seat in our village square. 'Would you like to hear a story?' she whispered.

We cheered as children do, then we jostled and gathered at her feet and waited breathlessly for her tale to unfold.

She arranged her cloak for a moment with hands that had seen better days, but she didn't seem old to us, for her voice was young and it smiled.

At first our parents watched her with suspicion in their eyes, but soon they stirred and continued with the business of their day.

This is the story that we heard.

'I'm going to tell you about a unicorn,' she stated.

We knew then that it was a story of make-believe, for unicorns aren't truly real, but her voice told us otherwise, and ever since, although I've told no one, my heart has believed every word.

'The unicorn's name was Benny,' she began. The dog stirred and thumped his tail. 'Benny lived with his mother Candela and his father Coraggio, amongst a wild and untouched herd. They were very beautiful.' She paused, and like mist in our eyes we could have sworn we heard thundering hooves.

'Candela's mane and tail,' she went on, 'flowed fully to the ground, catching wisps of breezes kissed by butterfly wings, and rippled like a gentle ocean. Coraggio had hooves of such strength there was nowhere he could not go. They lived in a forest of green and gold that was hidden from the outside world.'

Her eyes glowed and held each of ours as if challenging us to disbelieve. Then, sure we were listening and our hearts were on fire, she patted the dog's giant head gently and continued in a secret way.

'There was also, once, a girl.' Her voice grew hushed but then she spoke with power. 'The girl wandered far from home. She had a chum, a dog that she called Pud.'

'That rhymes with spud!' I cried, and the others laughed. The dog looked up and eyed me. I hung my head, but I swear he grinned.

The others called out. 'Was he a dog like yours? Was he also black and big?'

The traveller smiled as she held up a hand. 'Patience, have patience,' she urged.

A ripple of wind shook the trees above, and their branches slowly rocked. A leaf fluttered to land upon her shoulder.

'The girl's name,' she continued, 'was Rielle.'

Whining, the dog gazed up at her and placed a paw onto her shoe. Then he turned, and looked at us with eager amber eyes.

Nervously, we giggled. We knew *he* could not be Pud as this was a story of make-believe, and yet, one and all, our eyes locked on the giant at her feet. He lowered his massive head, then, as a loud murmur left his throat.

'Wait,' the traveller quickly said, 'let me tell you how it all began!'

Eagerly we leaned forward, like wind-strained trees.

'One night in a storm,' she announced, 'Rielle and Pud were lost.'

We shivered. 'Why were they lost?' we called. 'Were they all alone?'

'They were on a quest,' she replied, as if it made perfect sense.

'What is a quest?' we begged to know. 'What does it mean?'

'It's a search,' the traveller quickly answered. Her voice had become sad.

'What were they searching for?' we insisted. 'Were they scared?'

We each battered her with stubborn questions and watched unhappily as she stood as if to leave.

'Don't go,' we pleaded, 'stay to tell us more! We want to hear all about Pud, Rielle, and the unicorn.'

She eyed us, sat down, and let a moment of silence pass.

'All your questions will be answered,' she whispered, 'but if you want to hear my story you must listen carefully before the answers can become yours.'

We knew we had to know, so we nodded silently as if buttons held our lips. The leaf still sat upon her shoulder, its blue-green perfection glistening life-like in the sun.

She sighed. 'Rielle and Pud had run out of everything. They had no food or water and no place to sleep.' Her voice held and beckoned and trapped, one and all, we followed her like blind mice into a waiting cat's jaws.

'Ice and rain thrashed them, and mists made it impossible to see, yet high above, in the black night sky, the moon washed them in a blood red glow. Winds shrilled in choruses that were terrible in their madness and unbearable in their sadness.' She hesitated, raised her head and so did the dog.

We children huddled close, sneaking quick unhappy peeks over our shoulders, but there was nothing there that we could see. For several long moments we waited, our eyes rounded in anticipation, our hearts pounding with alarm. Would they survive the stormy night and would faithful Pud be alright?

'Suddenly,' she went on, 'the wind stopped howling and silence draped the mountain path. Rielle and Pud trembled, but was it mostly from cold or from fear?'

She paused, but I had fallen into the web she wove and her words had come to life. I watched as shapes walked and talked, and so it was, in that way, I got to meet the unicorns.

CHAPTER 1

Providence

Out of the silence, a crack of thunder boomed. Stunned, Rielle slipped and fell, rolling faster and faster into unknown things. With a thud, she finally stopped. Bruised and winded, she grimaced. Spitting mud from her teeth, she sat up. It was deadly dark. Tears took her by surprise but she brushed them away.

'Think, Rielle,' she muttered, 'think.'

Gathering her courage, she crawled around, stopping when she banged her head. 'Bear's breath!' she swore. Rubbing her face with one hand, she felt timidly around with the other.

'Hooley bondooley,' she snorted, sitting back on her heels, 'I think I'm inside some kind of tree! How did I do that?'

Still on the path, Pud sniffed for his mistress. She was gone! Distraught, he howled at the orange moon, sending echoes through the night.

'Where are you? Where are you?' he cried.

Rielle scrambled wildly, forgetting caution. 'Pud! I'm here Pud, in this tree, but be careful!'

Immediately, he leapt toward her voice with the precision of a clever dog, landing with a thump into her arms.

'Ouch!' Rielle bellowed as she lay flattened again. Pud didn't seem to notice as he danced a circle and licked her face.

'Bear's toes,' Rielle wheezed as she sat up, 'I feel like a squished plum. Do you know just how heavy you are, Pud?' She hugged him hard, though, and they huddled almost happily for a moment. 'We have each other,' she whispered, 'and I think we're safe for now.' Outside the tree-cave, lightning flashed and thunder roared.

'We've been lucky,' Rielle breathed. 'So far, nothing's crawled around in here, and let's hope it stays that way.' Pud licked her ear. 'I'm wet enough,' Rielle scolded, but she held him closer anyway.

For long moments they crouched helplessly. 'I suppose all we can do is sleep,' Rielle finally muttered, as she nestled next to the dog.

Pud soon snored as only a dog can, but hungrier and colder than she'd ever been, Rielle dozed with strange, fitful dreams that held her captive and were more than real. She and Pud had roamed for the longest time but they'd never spent a night inside a tree before!

No matter how long a night may feel or how bad it is, the morning always comes. Like a blanket of embroidered dust, it crept with a salting of newborn sun and a peppering of lukewarm air to sprinkle dew through the dawn. Light poked Rielle in the face, catching the edges of her eyes and forcing her half awake. She had been dreaming.

Safe in her old home, dancing in the fragrant garden under sprays of moonbeam, she was wearing her favourite dress. The fabric matched the stars of sky and night, and her hair shone; silky dark, clean and bright. Best of all, she hadn't been dancing alone. She was laughing and twirling and dancing like she'd never danced before.

Jolting up, Rielle looked around. It was dim inside the tree but fingers of light were climbing its branches. The storm was gone.

'Hooley dooley,' she grimaced, 'I hope that awful smell isn't you, Pud?'

She sneezed and tried to move her legs. For worrying moments she wondered if she'd been hurt in the fall, but it was just Pud sprawled everywhere and crushing her legs to pins and needles. She poked him. Pud opened an eye, looked at her, shut it, and continued to snore.

Rielle frowned. 'Come on, wake up, we have to get out of here!'

Pud opened his eyes. His tan eyebrows wiggled and he nudged her arm with his cold, wet nose.

Rielle grinned, despite their troubles. 'It doesn't matter what happens, you think everything is a big adventure.'

Pud sneezed happily as his tail crashed and thumped a dance.

'You are my *best* friend,' Rielle said, smiling.

She stood up stiffly. 'But let's get out of here. I want to get clean, and I'm so hungry I could scream.'

Pud handed her his paw and solemnly agreed.

'This way,' Rielle urged, noticing a large hole high in the tree's side. 'This must be what we fell through.'

Scrambling, she helped Pud out first, which was no easy task. Then, finally, after several tries, Rielle, too, stumbled into the day.

It was hard to believe that the morning was a sister to the night before, as silvery dust motes rolled through shafts of sunlight in the soft and sugary air. Peace breathed around them with a sigh.

The tree creaked as if to say goodbye. Rielle patted its groaning wood.

'Thank you, tree,' she whispered, before stepping onto the battered path. No sooner had she done so than Pud leapt in front of her.

'What?' Rielle frowned.

Pud howled. Rielle turned around.

'Lion's fangs!' Rielle pulled back. 'Look where we are!' Not two strides away the path was broken, falling into a deep abyss. The tree had saved their lives!

'Oh, Pud,' she whispered, white-faced, 'we could have gone to the bottom of that.' The chasm had an end somewhere, but she couldn't see it, hard as she tried. It made her dizzy yet she couldn't tear her eyes away.

Just then, as an impolite interruption to Rielle's gloomy thoughts, a finger of wind pounced on the hat she wore and plucked it right off the top of her head.

'Hey, you,' Rielle called angrily to the wind, 'give it back!'

The hat relaxed for a twinkling moment, suspended in the air, but as Rielle lunged to grab it, the wind teased and twirled it out of reach. The tree's leaves jiggled and a butterfly danced straight past her nose.

Rielle loved her hat. It kept her head warm and dry

and it was her favourite colour. Sometimes she used it to gather fruit and nuts, but best of all, it was given to her one long-ago day by a dear friend. She wasn't about to lose it to a cheeky wisp of airplay! Forgetting the black-bottomed gorge, she leapt clear of the perilous path and pounced with quick annoyance. But the wind had become a hand and it sent her hat flying into the nearby forest.

Immediately, Pud galloped after it, barking wildly as he ran.

Rielle didn't pause to think. 'You can't have it!' she bellowed to the wind as she plunged after Pud. Charging through prickly bushes and sliding over hidden logs, she suddenly realised she couldn't hear her dog. She stopped.

'It will be my fault if something's happened to him,' she breathed. Again she began to run.

'Pud! Pud!' she called, as worry put eagles on her heels. Picking up speed on a grass-grown path, she ran so fast that she nearly missed the signs and almost collided with a boulder. She swerved, and with luck, as she saw it then, she burst upon a tiny clearing. Her panting breath rasped through the forest as she slid to a halt and took stock of where she was.

Pickled in a dappled light of green and gold, and nestled in such quiet that it hit her like a noise, the clearing was unlike anywhere she'd ever been before. A mist of velvet mosses crept like gentle caterpillars up and down the trunks of trees with some tree roots so large they broke the soil and then returned, twisted and entwined. Ancient lichen trickled gently over rocks as dragonflies dozed lightly on the wing. A small brown tortoise, seeing her, peeked timidly from within its shell. A tiny stream offered breathy secrets, then muttered on and gurgled by as an elfin bird piped a call and received a distant answer. Lazy sunlight filtered the thick tree growth, leaving strips of gloom on the silky wet grass. Rielle was the loudest thing in the glen.

Pud was there, standing right in the middle of the clearing.

'Pud!' Rielle shouted, relieved, and the precious silence was broken again. She cringed, her eyes flashing an apology to the forest cathedral.

Pud didn't seem to hear her, and that was odd.

'Pud, are you alright?' Rielle whispered, tiptoeing toward him.

Pud stood with his tail high, his head tilted and a wrinkled brow.

'Pud?' Rielle breathed.

He didn't answer. He was watching something, but there was nothing there that she could see. Straining her eyes to see beyond the clearing, the forest offered nothing. It was then that Rielle heard the voice. At least she thought it was a voice. The hairs on her neck stood on end.

Pud barked.

Casually, peering through the corners of her eyes, Rielle cleared her throat and made a show of standing tall.

'Did you say something, Pud?' she whispered, but he kept staring at empty space.

What should she do? Pud never behaved like this! Again she heard the voice, but this time there was no mistaking what it said.

'You have big eyebrows,' it murmured in a soft, gritty voice.

'You have a funny face,' Pud yipped.

Rielle's heart pounded. She checked the ground, but just like the air, it was empty. 'Come on Pud,' she urged, 'let's get out of here.'

Pud didn't budge.

Rielle held back panic. 'I'm not going to look over there.' But even as she muttered the words she just had to peek. Pud hadn't moved. Prickly with the need to escape, Rielle perched ready to run.

'Who are you talking to, Pud?' she begged.

Again Pud ignored her. He stood his ground. 'You have my mistress' hat,' he grunted.

The other voice quipped. 'She may have to get it herself.'

'That's it,' Rielle spat, 'I don't like this! What is it, Pud? What can you see, and who is it you're talking to?' She asked the question, but in her heart, she wasn't sure she wanted to know. Her mind raced, thoughts colliding. *Should I be afraid? Should I run?* But she couldn't leave without her dog and he wasn't moving for anything!

Rielle told herself the stealthy stirrings in the air were just her imagination but, like slow, creeping fingers, the silence in the glade grew deeper and she couldn't hear a sound. Helplessly, she looked over at her best friend and promised herself not to yell at him again. After all, it wasn't his fault they were lost and that she was scared. Through all the times of thick and thin, he'd always been her one true friend.

'I'm sorry, Pud,' she whispered, 'I don't understand what's going on, so please, can we go?'

Like a pattering of kitten's paws, dots of light began to dance and tumble and next the sun began to shine just so. Then, like a sudden marvel, Rielle saw what she hadn't seen before. She stared, blinked, shut her eyes, opened them, blinked again and gazed in wonder. She could see it clearly now!

CHAPTER 2

I tell no lies, I am true

At the same height as her dog, and looking him squarely in the eyes, stood a little horse. Its coat was shiny, silky white and it had big green eyes. Right in the middle of its forehead was a pointed horn.

Rielle held her breath.

'Oh,' she exclaimed, 'you're a unicorn!'

Trees sighed again, leaves wiggled on boughs, a bird trilled and the stream moved on, as butterflies danced past in pairs. Then the dainty creature, not a horse at all, bowed to Pud and calmly looked her way.

'Yes, I am,' it replied in the gritty voice. With spry dignity it poised the hat neatly on the tip of its horn, and then, stepping high, went and stood in front of her.

Breathless, Rielle took back her hat.

'Thank you,' she whispered, as her heart skipped a beat.

'I'm Benny,' replied the unicorn, 'and I'm pleased to meet you.' Then with a bow, a blink and a sigh, he turned to walk away.

'Wait!' Rielle called. She couldn't just let him go. After all, he was a unicorn.

He turned his head to look at her, his eyes aloof, calm and cool.

Rielle struggled for words. Was this really true? Her quest had been long and strange, but she had never seen something like this before. What did you say to a unicorn, and why was this all happening to her?

'Um, well,' she began, 'I haven't thanked you for finding my hat.'

The unicorn nodded.

'My name is Rielle,' she continued, 'and I hope Pud didn't offend you. He was just doing his job, you understand, protecting me.'

Benny waited.

Rielle blustered. 'I'm sorry I yelled. I mean, I couldn't see anything. I didn't think there was anything there. I hope I haven't insulted you and I'm sorry if I have.'

The little unicorn tossed his head. Peeking with twinkling eyes through his silken forelock, he flicked his mane and called, 'I know where there's food!'

Then with a kick of his heels, he galloped into the forest.

Rielle and Pud looked at each other for a fleeting second but Benny had said 'food' and that was enough for them. Once again that morning, they were chasing and hot-tailing for all their worth. The forest opened its arms, to shut quietly behind them as they passed.

Swift hooves and strong legs let the unicorn gallop like the wind. Pud, too, ran easily, jumping logs like he was born to it. But Rielle wasn't made for hurdling like a deer. She ran fit to bust, grateful for her long pants and sturdy boots, but she was no unicorn or dog, and was soon left far behind. Puffed, she stopped and looked around.

'Hooley dooley,' she gaped, 'where the blazes am I now?'

The forest rang with bird song and rustled with breezes stepping through trees. Rielle shivered, afraid without Pud by her side. The air was clammy with quivering undercurrents and a strange mood, as if the forest watched her every step. Taking a breath, Rielle whistled piercingly for Pud. Birds scattered at the sudden noise, but Pud didn't appear.

'First that storm and then my hat,' Rielle grumbled, looking anxiously around, 'and then Pud finds a unicorn!' Unwillingly, for a moment, she grinned. 'Gosh, it was a unicorn. It was truly real, wasn't it?' She frowned. 'I believed it when it said 'food' but now I'm lost and here... wherever this is, and all without my dog.'

The night in the tree felt like years ago. Why had their journey brought them here? Misgivings and strange feelings of déjà vu flushed her blood, and warned her that this was a place of no return.

Loneliness encased Rielle's travel-weary heart. Bleakly, she sat down on an old log. Taking her hat and cloak off, she looked back at the way she'd come, but nothing moved and there was no clear path, just bushes and wild spongy grass.

Rielle whistled for Pud again, but he did not appear.

'Oh Pud,' she whispered, her head sinking to her chest, 'am I ever going to see you again?'

Something tapped her shoulder. It was a tree branch brushing her, and fruit weighed heavily on its limbs. Rielle glanced around. Ancient trees stretched above her head, all bearing different kinds of fruit. She laughed and grabbed an apple, bit into it, then checked the core for wormy bits but the apple was the best she'd ever eaten and so she ate six. *This had to be the place where the food grew! The unicorn didn't lie, so Pud might be alright!*

Rielle crammed pears and peaches into her mouth, then wiped the juice from her chin and clothes. Almost content, she looked up to judge the time of day, but something caught her eye. She frowned. White fog drifted behind the thick of the forest.

'Mists!' Rielle spat. 'They creep around and grab you until you become lost or... worse.' Hurriedly, she put her cloak and hat back on. It wouldn't do to get damp and cold again.

Quickly, she glanced at the forest, but even as she did so, goose bumps pricked her arms. This was no mist!

From behind the trees there stepped a whole herd of unicorns. Grazing with watchful, gentle eyes and floating with silvery strides, their manes and tails rippled like a field of corn. They stepped carefully, so as not to crush a living thing with their hooves. In the dappled light they looked like spirits or eerie ghosts, yet they dazzled with their silent beauty, white light surrounding them in a glow.

There were so many! Rielle's heart thumped. They hadn't seen her - of that she was sure - so she held her breath, afraid to move. She wished Pud were there to see them.

'Don't let them go or take fright and run,' she breathed. 'Let them stay, please let them stay.'

Suddenly, they stopped grazing. As one, they looked up. It wasn't her they'd noticed but something else. Rielle turned. A little unicorn cantered into the glade. It was Benny, followed by Pud.

The herd trilled with a call of joy.

'Oh,' Rielle gasped, 'how hauntingly they cry.'

Again and again the unicorns trilled and, with each call, an echo would quiver, making her wait and want to hear it once more.

Benny trilled loudly in reply then skidded sharply in front of Rielle.

'I knew you'd find food,' he cried, 'and don't worry, Pud has eaten too.' He cocked his head. 'I have to go. They're waiting!' With a huge buck, he ran to the herd.

Rielle watched spellbound, as all of the unicorns came forward and, one by one, gently tapped horns with Benny. The tapping filled the glen with harmony, odd and mesmerising in its beauty.

Pud trotted sheepishly to Rielle. Sitting at her feet, he hid his face with his paw.

'Oh Pud,' Rielle giggled as she hugged him hard. 'I thought you were gone for ever that time.'

Pud sneezed and licked her nose.

'Listen, Pud,' Rielle breathed, 'they make a kind of music. What do you think it means?'

A unicorn standing nearby stepped from the herd and stood beside her.

'Whenever a unicorn returns,' he whispered, watching her with earnest eyes, 'especially from far away, each member of the herd gently taps their forehead or horn, which makes a kind of humming sound. It removes the shadows of the outside world and makes us unified. In that way, our hearts stay free of doubt or fear, and we remain true and hold our power. It keeps us strong and as one,' he concluded. 'It is the *Ritual of Return.*'

'Oh, how wonderful,' Rielle exclaimed, a pang of longing stabbing her heart. 'How lucky to be a unicorn!'

The forest soon filled with vibrant tunes. Enthralled, Rielle and Pud warmed to the joyful sounds. Rielle forgot that she was lost. She forgot she wanted to wash mud from her face and clothes. Pud sat by her as she idly plucked his ears and together they watched and listened, lulled by the sounds of the unicorn herd. Around them, the forest sparkled in a flood of green and gold, borrowed from forest mosses and trees, filtered sun and coloured leaves. The sounds soothed Rielle. She grew drowsy and then she dozed.

'Rielle! Oh, Rielle!'

Rielle woke with a start, staring straight into a pair of twinkling green eyes. Whiskers tickled her face. Delighted, she remembered... they were in a mysterious forest with a unicorn herd.

'Good, she's awake,' Benny smiled.

Rielle sat up.

With a serious face, Benny went on. 'Rielle, I would like you to meet my mother Candela, for the light of candles in the dark, and my father Coraggio, for bravery and strength.'

The forest was shadowing where Rielle sat, but the unicorns lit the air with a glow. Good Pud sat respectfully at attention as two large unicorns with velvet eyes looked sweetly at Rielle and eternal wisdom.

Rielle felt very shy. Up close, their beauty was daunting and she did not feel worthy. The warm air of their breath was sweet and grassy, their eyes were huge and thickly lashed and their skin rippled like silk. Coraggio had a mighty crest and Candela shimmered and shone.

'Hello,' Rielle whispered, tremulous and awed.

Candela and Coraggio bowed their heads in greeting and then they did a mysterious thing. Gently, they touched their horns to her forehead, tapped just once, and wordless, they turned and quietly walked away.

Rielle's breath caught in her throat. Her forehead was warm where she had been tapped, and with trembling fingers she touched the spot. It tingled, and the skin felt rough and warm. Without a word to anyone, Rielle dashed to the pond nearby. She almost didn't dare to look but she had to know, so bracing herself she looked at her reflection. A mark was etched upon her brow that was roughly shaped like a little star.

'What does it mean?' she gasped.

Benny looked fully at her. 'Now you belong,' he whispered, as if all along he knew her mind.

The day was fading in the glen as spirals of sun-slant pierced the forest in shafts of fading glory. The sun was shifting to evening post, preparing for the night and bed.

Rielle pulled out her trusty cooking things from her small travel sack and built a fire with castaway sticks, then cooked a meal made from herbs and wild roots she'd found in the forest. She shared her meal with Pud.

It was lumpy, but hot and very tasty. Pud slurped while Rielle thought.

With trembling fingers she touched her brow again, and knew somehow that her life was changed. The star-scar was strangely familiar already, as if it had always been there. Although she didn't understand, there was mystery and prophecy in the very air she breathed. She marvelled, and kept looking at the unicorns. *Now you belong*, he'd said. There was no going back, she knew.

As the last light trickled away, Rielle thought about the howling horror of the night before. Gratitude flooded through her as she shivered at their close call. She would never take trees for granted again! Pud came close then, and placed his cool nose on her hand. He knew when she was afraid, lonely, feeling lost, or sad. A huge grey owl scooted past them, followed closely by another. The owls met and clung to the same tree branch then hooted harmonies at the night.

Dusk was done and night creatures stirred.

Rielle whistled softly to Pud. 'Come on chum,' she murmured, 'help me find a place to sleep for the night.'

Together, they explored in the quiet, growing dark, searching the little glade, until they found an excellent place. Beneath a bank, a natural hollow made something of a cave. It was lined with soft lichen and dry moss.

'Perfect,' Rielle smiled. 'It's cosy, but large enough for us to squeeze in.'

Together they snuggled, and with full bellies, a feeling of safety crept through their minds. Rielle noticed the unicorn herd grazing quietly, never far from sight.

'I'm not a bit sleepy,' she sighed, 'and there's the whole long night ahead. Look, Pud, have you ever seen such big, bright stars?'

Pud looked up and watched with her, then lay down and placed his paws upon her feet.

'You know Pud,' Rielle mused, 'when I dozed before, I had the strangest dream.' She looked at Pud and he looked back, listening carefully with a furrowed brow.

'I dreamed,' she continued, 'that I rode on the wings of a butterfly. I thought the wind told me something as it swept towards us. I heard flowers sing as they bloomed, and I know this sounds silly, but I think the earth breathed. There was fire also, but it wasn't burning, it was as if... well... as if it was a fire in the belly of all things! Everything was perfect... I felt it in here,' she tapped her heart and then paused to remember more.

'Then we passed over some mountains and rivers, and at last the butterfly spoke to me, but all she said was: '*We are here.*' I got off her wings, and there in front of me was a gigantic door. It had something written on it in funny writing. Let me see if I can remember. I think it read mor... something. No. It was mort something. No, it was mortal. No, that wasn't it; it was a longer word.' She wrinkled her brow.

'I've got it! It was mort... al... ity. Yes, that's it. Mortality. What a funny word.' She sighed. 'I knew a secret while I was in the dream. I understood something, but I can't remember what.'

Rielle absently patted Pud while she wracked her brain.

'What do you think mortality means, Pud?'

Before Pud had a chance to answer, Benny came over, tiptoeing in an exaggerated slow walk, as if to prove he could. He didn't say a thing at first; he just began to make small circles. First he walked around to the left, and then to the right, and just as Rielle was wondering what the blazes he was doing, he plonked himself down beside their den.

Pud walked over and licked him on the nose, then returned to sit by Rielle.

After more shuffling and shunting, Benny finally settled with a flick of his tail and a toss of his head. He looked at Rielle boldly, staring her in the eye.

Rielle felt awkward at his no-nonsense gaze.

Benny didn't hold back. 'Have you run away?' he asked, with open curiosity.

Rielle wasn't expecting that. She hedged, still not sure how to speak to a creature that she thought belonged in myth and legend.

'What do you mean?' she gruffly asked.

'You know what I mean, Rielle,' challenged Benny, 'you must be lost, or far from home. I haven't seen anyone like you here before.'

Rielle opened her eyes wide. *She* wasn't the one who was different or unusual in any way. There were plenty of people in the world, but where did one see a unicorn?

'Run away?' She shook her head, answering sharply. 'No, I wouldn't call it that.'

Benny nodded and waited quietly. 'Oh,' was all he said.

Long, open moments went by as owls hooted loudly

overhead and small night noises made creaking sounds.

'I don't want you to judge me,' stammered Rielle.

Benny opened his eyes. 'What was that?' he grunted. 'I was dozing for a bit. Judge you? That was the furtherest thing from my mind.'

'You mean furthest,' corrected Rielle, knowing she was being bossy, and not very nice.

'Furtherest... furthest.' Benny rolled his eyes. 'The last thing I was doing was judging you, I promise.'

Rielle glanced around the moonlit glen. 'I've been in many places,' she murmured, 'but this must be the most beautiful forest I've ever, ever seen.'

Benny yawned in open-mouthed relish and made a puzzled face. 'Look at me, Rielle,' he pressed, 'I'm a unicorn. Do you know anything about unicorns?'

Rielle shrugged her shoulders. What did he mean? Of course she didn't know anything about unicorns! Why would she know anything about unicorns? No one knew anything about unicorns where she had come from! What sort of answer was he looking for? She knew she was being rude, but in times of bewilderment she couldn't seem to help herself so she just shrugged, frowned, and made a pouting mouth.

Benny tilted his head at her. 'You don't happen to know the riddle of unicorns then, by any chance, Rielle?'

She still wasn't sure what he wanted. One minute they were talking about her, then next Benny was talking about riddles. With a quirky expression on his face, Benny waited for her reply.

'Well, until today,' she began haughtily, hoping to

appear clever, 'I didn't know that unicorns were real.'
She paused and absently hugged Pud. 'So, I suppose,'
she continued, very pleased with herself, 'the riddle of
unicorns is that you really do exist after all?'

With a chuckle, Benny just shook his head. 'Nope,' he
grinned, 'that's no riddle.'

It dawned on Rielle that she should be honoured and
privileged to be in this special place, sitting and talking
with a little unicorn in an enchanting forest amongst a
whole herd.

'Well,' she stammered in a small, embarrassed voice,
'I'd really like to know the riddle of unicorns, if you'd like
to tell me.' She looked at Benny and her heart skipped a
beat. His gaze was so intense that it was almost sinister.

'I can't *tell* you, Rielle,' he whispered solemnly. 'I just
wondered if you knew, that's all.'

Rielle felt her heart tighten. Suddenly, more than
anything, she wanted to know. 'Can I find out?' she
begged. 'Will I ever know?'

Benny, however, just sneezed and grinned. 'Sneezes
are such fun, don't you think?' He beamed cheekily then
continued. 'So, tell me Rielle, have you travelled far?'

Rielle was annoyed at the change of pace. 'You just
changed the subject and anyway, I think you asked me
that before.'

'No I didn't,' Benny answered calmly. 'Before, I asked
you if you'd run away.'

'Okay then, no, I haven't run away.' Rielle scowled
and then grumbled guardedly, 'I... I've just walked a
long, long way for a long, long time, that's all!' Who was

he to ask her questions? She refused to meet the little unicorn's eye.

'I wish you'd tell me why,' sighed Benny.

Rielle gave up. It *was* his forest, she supposed. She was the intruder, after all. Glancing at him, she saw only kindness and deep concern in his sweet green eyes.

'I... I don't like to talk about it. It makes me sad,' she mumbled.

Benny looked kindly at her. 'Maybe I can help?' he replied.

Rielle hesitated, fear clouding her heart.

'I've never spoken about it to a living soul,' she finally whispered, boldness colouring her voice. 'Well, except for Pud. Pud knows all there is to know but he never laughs or thinks I'm foolish.' She scowled.

'I promise I won't laugh, Rielle,' Benny answered softly and sincerely.

For a long time, Rielle sat in silence, wondering how she should reply. The whisperings of the night told her that owls crooned and night creatures grunted and squeaked. A lively breeze chattered with leaves, making them rustle and jig. Close by, a waterfall tinkled as it met a jumbled destiny. Rielle opened her mouth to speak, but closed it several times.

Pud snored and Benny waited.

Rielle loathed going back to where it all began, this wandering and this journey, the quest that she had chosen! Anyhow, she mentally shrugged; she was used to it by now, so what did it matter how long she'd been travelling, or how far? She looked up past the brim of her small cave as if the answer waited there, then through the canopy of forest growth, branches shifted and she saw the moon. Beside it was a simple star, which blinked and looked right back at her, then seemed to nod at her to speak.

'I think,' Rielle said, rushing her words, 'I think my heart is broken.' It sounded silly when she said it out loud. Quickly, she checked Benny's face. It wouldn't do if he sneered or laughed. Benny, however, sat with half-closed eyes, almost as if he wasn't listening.

Tears in Rielle's eyes marched with tremors in her throat. She coughed and glanced at Benny again, but his eyes and face rested quietly, and he wasn't watching her at all.

Encouraged, Rielle went on. 'I'm sad, you see, and I don't think my heart can mend.'

Benny looked at a spot on the ground and nodded.

Rielle gulped a breath of air. 'I wasn't always like this,' she persisted with courage, as memories made words stop in her throat. With an effort she continued. 'But now, well, now I guess, I'm all unhappy pieces… inside, you know?'

She took a deep breath. 'It's me and Pud on the road now. That's what we do. Wandering has become our way of life. I… well, I suppose I'm searching for something,' she finished in a rush.

With a look, she dared Benny to snigger. She was fierce with anger and felt foolish for baring her soul as she never had to a stranger before. Pride made her cheeks burn and scald and she prepared to defend herself if he laughed, but Benny didn't move.

A long silence followed. Consolingly, Pud licked Rielle's ear. She didn't notice.

'You see me, Benny, as I am now,' Rielle finally whispered. 'Bits of me are left behind, and bits of me are here, but none of me is whole.'

Benny didn't ask any questions, although he longed to know. He understood there was much, much more to her story, but he couldn't make her tell him unless she wanted to. A great many thoughts rushed through his mind, but for now they were best unsaid. He knew the most important thing, though. Rielle was wandering on a quest, obviously seeking something important, or searching for something stolen or lost.

Shifty winds rustled. Trickles of moonlight dribbled on the ground.

'What about your parents?' Benny finally asked. 'Won't they be missing you?'

'No,' Rielle whispered in a rush. 'No, they won't! *I have no one...* except for Pud.' Even as she said it, she touched the star-scar on her brow.

So Benny... dearest little unicorn... asked nothing more. Instead, he laid his dainty head tenderly upon Rielle's shoulder and for many moments, he rested there. A giant tear dropped from his eye to lie upon his cheek. He sighed and the herd sighed. Rielle was understood.

'Actually,' Rielle went on defiantly, 'I've come to like my walking and my wandering. Well, that is, until the other night when we met that terrible storm.'

Benny frowned. 'In all your wandering, you've only met one storm?'

'Oh we've been through lots of storms,' Rielle quickly replied, 'but nothing like that one. What I mean is that we've never become lost like this before.' She looked around. 'I mean, we've never met unicorns.' Her cheeks began to burn. 'I mean, not that it isn't nice *now*, but we were so scared and lost, and the path that we thought was safe was all crumbled and broken. And there was this huge cliff that we nearly fell off. And… and, if we hadn't been lucky and fallen inside a tree,' she shuddered, 'who knows where Pud and I would be?'

Benny chuckled.

Rielle looked shocked. 'What's so funny about that?' she cried.

Benny's grin grew wider. 'That would be Old Poky that caught you,' he whispered cheekily. 'He only lets *bad* people fall into the abyss!'

Rielle gasped, stricken.

Benny looked despairingly at her, wondering if she had a sense of humour. 'Oh, there now, I'm only joking,' he sighed. 'I do that sometimes you know.'

'I suppose what I'm trying to say,' Rielle continued, with a hurt look at Benny, 'is that I've wandered so much and walked so far, that this… this, um, journey, now feels normal for Pud and me.' She hesitated for a moment then timidly asked. 'Do you think that makes me strange, Benny?' She looked fearfully at him. Then with a pained expression, she finally asked, 'Do you think I'm daft?'

Benny blinked at her several times. 'Daft? Oh, that!' he exclaimed. 'You aren't daft, you're just *LASED*.'

'*LASED*?' Rielle asked. What word was this? She

shook her head at him, puzzled and confused. 'I've never heard of that before.'

Benny looked back with cool green eyes as he plucked a juicy blade of grass, squishing it in his mouth with dainty teeth and lips.

'What's LASED?' Rielle repeated. 'I've never heard of it. I don't think it's a real word, unless it's one that unicorns use.'

Benny plucked another blade of grass, sucking it like a noodle. He rolled his eyes at the tasty treat then said, *'Lost All Sense of Eventual Direction. L.A.S.E.D.'*

'Oh,' Rielle sighed with relief, 'is that all? It doesn't sound so bad.' It seemed she wasn't daft, she just had LASED.

'All?' Benny cried, with flashing eyes. 'All? LASED is big, maybe even huge!'

Rielle caught her breath, and her throat went tight. A minute ago she had started to think that things might be alright. 'It sounds worse than being daft,' she gasped, and burst into hot, frightened tears. 'It sounds like I've got some horrible, creeping, sickening disease!'

Pud sat up bristling. 'I've never made her cry,' he grunted, and sat closer to his mistress, watching Benny with a wary eye.

Benny sucked another stem of grass then casually replied.

'I didn't make her cry dear Pud, LASED did. You see, it is the biggest, saddest, most inhuman state of all affairs.'

Rielle glared round-eyed, in disbelief. She wasn't daft; instead she just had the biggest, saddest, most inhuman state of all affairs, and it was something she'd never even heard of before! She felt helpless.

'What will I do? What should I do? Tell me Benny, what should I do?' *Was the little unicorn really a friend?* She had trusted him but things looked grim.

'Well,' Benny replied, 'for starters, don't listen to well-meaning folk when they tell you to *move on,* or to *get a grip,* or say to you, *carry on old chap, pick up your chin and get on with it!* It's total nonsense when they say... *cheer up, don't be absurd,* and double stupid to expect that you remain *undeterred.* You see, there's no such thing as *stiff-upper-lip, gee-up or snap out of it!* Those are the words that people use, because they either just don't care, or don't know what else to say!'

Benny was very matter-of-fact, and as if to make his point more clearly, he nodded his head several times before he carried on.

'All that stuff never works. Pain doesn't wish or talk away; it must be fixed! I mean, do you tell a broken leg, *just move on and walk away,* or do you tell a bleeding arm, *look here arm, why don't you mend?* And of course there's a swollen eye. Would you say to it, *cheer up, pretend you see and all will be fine.* No! You have to splint the leg to fix the break, bind the arm with nice clean cotton wool, put an ice pack on the eye, and then make sure they have time to fix!'

Benny paused and breathed in deeply. His chin was high and his eyes were unwavering, and they could tell he wasn't finished yet.

'Feelings are no different,' he continued, 'they have

to be mended and not ignored, otherwise they simply never change.'

Rielle noticed that the herd had tiptoed to stand and listen by her little den. Like guardians they stood as Benny spoke, nodding sagely now and then. Swishing their tails and tossing their manes, they waited for him to go on.

The forest shifted with a chill night air as if pondering his words.

'Anyhow, I have an idea,' Benny announced. He stood up and shook himself. It was obvious that he was preparing for something big. He paused, and the wait was more than anyone could stand.

Pud uncurled and sat upright and stiff. The herd craned their necks to listen, then flared their nostrils and sniffed. The family of owls flew softly down, settled and perched on the bank, and Rielle could have sworn that trees bent over, to quietly listen in. They waited - the herd, the dog, the forest beasts and Rielle - for Benny's big idea.

Benny stretched slowly forward and then slowly backward. He yawned and shook himself from head to tail, then with urgency, scratched a small spot on his chest. At last he gave one great shake that forced neatness on his curly mane and tail, as everyone watched and waited with growing expectation.

CHAPTER 3

I fear neither the dark nor the unknown

'I think it's time,' Benny began at last, 'to go on a questing journey of my own.' He looked around and watched as the crowd grasped the idea.

Coraggio and Candela's eyes met. Benny was becoming a fine unicorn.

The suspense was too much for Rielle. 'Where would you go?' she timidly queried, asking the question on everyone's mind.

'Well,' Benny answered slowly, 'I'm not sure what I'll find when I get there, mind you, but I think it's my duty to go and look.' He paused, reflecting, then secretly whispered. 'I need to go to the land of Wish.'

'Oooh,' crooned the owls, blinking hard.

'Ohhh,' the herd groaned, and some pawed the ground.

Benny nodded in silent agreement. The thought was uttered; it now had form, and his weighty mission was more than just words. The silence reached out into the forest like a hand seeking the unknown.

Benny took a deep breath. 'I need to find the Tower of Dreams.' He stood quietly to think it through.

An owl screeched and the silence deepened, as if no one had words to voice their concern. Then everyone seemed to shuffle at once. *Wish, it was known, was only for the brave!* The herd was nervous and some trilled out loud.

Hackles had risen on Pud's neck with an instinct he could not explain. He took a step closer to the little unicorn, craning to hear Benny speak. He wanted to understand, as he sensed that this information was important in many ways.

Rielle shivered, not knowing why. 'Wish?' she asked.

'It's another land,' Benny replied.

Before anyone else had a chance to speak, Pud asked, 'What's a Tower of Dreams?'

Benny glanced at the herd. Candela nodded to his silent question.

'The Tower of Dreams,' Benny replied, carefully choosing his words, 'is in the land of Wish, beyond the purple mountains and somewhat to the right.' He looked around. He had their full attention, so he continued on. 'The last unicorn to go there was my mother, Candela, a very long time ago. She went there for the answer to a puzzle, and that is why I want to go too.'

The moon peeped out from under dark clouds, shooting radiant beams to the huddled crowd. Like black, brooding statues they all stood, with little Benny as the centre point.

Benny lowered his voice to Pud. 'Wish is an ever changing land because it exists from the minds of humans.'

Rielle sat up taller. There was a place that humans made with their minds? This was captivating stuff. She wanted to go there straight away! However, Benny was still talking.

'I've heard that it can be a wonderful place, but it's well known for its hidden traps. Even the wise are challenged there, but for the unprepared,' Benny rolled his eyes, 'it's full of snares.' He gazed at the circle of friends gathered in the glen, and saw deep concern buried in their eyes.

Candela nodded. 'Anything is possible there,' she trilled. 'Just remember that.'

Pud furrowed his brow, still looking confused. 'How can something be real,' he asked, 'if it is only a thought, or in someone's mind? Does it mean you can touch things there, or how does it work?'

The herd shifted again, still restless and disturbed.

'Humans,' began Benny pensively, choosing his words with care, 'build ideas with their minds, it seems, and there's nothing wrong with that. In fact it's kind of clever and can be very good.'

He looked at Candela. She blinked.

'That is,' he continued, 'if ideas are born from truth and kindness and honest things, but alas!' Benny paused, peeking from under his forelock and tilting his head at Rielle.

'Please don't take offence Rielle, but humans can be selfish, greedy, filled with envy and confusion, and what they think they really want they often take without a care or thought. They can be careless with their free will, causing a troubled fate.'

Pud and Rielle made anxious faces.

'Wish is only real because of the thoughts of humans,'

Benny went on, 'but the good news is that the Tower of Dreams is no illusion. It's very real!'

'Oh,' cut in Pud, speaking slowly to gather his thoughts, 'but what does it do?'

Benny furrowed his brow and swished his tail. 'Do?' he stamped a hoof and arched his neck then lowered his head to where Pud sat. 'Do you mean the Tower of Dreams?' Pud simply nodded.

'The Tower of Dreams is where Hope lives,' Benny promptly replied as if everyone knew, 'and I need to speak with Hope.'

Pud tilted his head first one way and then the other. 'So,' Pud quizzed with his large tan eyebrows furrowed, 'what does Hope do?'

The herd shifted, tossing their heads and gently trilling, almost in a chuckle. Benny quickly glanced at Candela then kindly, he replied.

'Well Pud, I am told that Hope knows all kinds of things. Hope can tell why people are sad or why it is they are bad, but Hope can be hard to find, so the easiest way to find Hope is to go to where Hope lives.'

'But,' Pud asked, not letting it go, 'aren't you a unicorn? Unicorns aren't sad or bad, so why do you need to speak with Hope?'

'Ah, yes, I see what you mean,' smiled Benny, 'and of course you're right, but you see, Pud, I'm not going for myself. I need to solve a puzzle but it's for someone else.' He paused. Everyone waited.

'It's for Rielle,' Benny finished with a flourish.

Rielle craned her neck and her eyes nearly popped.

What on earth was Benny on about?

'Rielle?' asked Pud.

'Yes, dear Pud. I need to ask Hope if Rielle still has a dream. Hope will tell me if Rielle's dreams are all gone, as she believes.'

The herd's eyes all turned to Rielle. Their velvet depths showed real concern.

'Rielle has a heart that is truly broken and may never mend,' Benny stated. 'So, I have decided to find Hope for her, because she might never find Hope to ask for herself.'

At this last revelation the herd gasped. Looking downcast, one and all, they shook their heads.

Rielle felt bewildered and small. In fact she felt worse than when Benny had told her she had LASED. Now everyone was looking at her with long, sad faces and dejected eyes, as if she had the plague.

'But,' Benny exclaimed loudly, 'that doesn't make Rielle a bad person, Pud. No, not at all!' The herd pricked their ears. Pud moved closer so as not to miss a single word.

'Bad people hurt other people,' Benny continued, 'because they're selfish and unkind. Bad people only do what's good for them and then they walk away and don't look back again. Bad people live their lives with no regard for anyone else.'

Benny nudged Pud with his nose, then stomped his tiny hooves as if to make a point. The herd snorted and shied and the forest swayed as trees shook their limbs.

'I think,' Benny murmured, as he peered at Rielle with one eye shut, 'that Rielle once brimmed and flowed with laughter. I think that no matter where she walks or how hard the road, Rielle carries on. I think Rielle is brave but hides behind her lack of trust.'

Pud looked at Benny with open warmth. 'Yes,' he sighed, 'I see now.' Then with his amber eyes shining, Pud made an honest plea. 'Please, Benny,' Pud implored, 'ask Hope to make Rielle happy, like she used to be.'

Rielle was bashful and deeply moved. They were all cheering, just for her! It was true; she didn't let her guard down, as the law of survival was to trust no one.

'So,' asked Pud with determined curiosity, 'when will you go on your journey? Will it be soon?'

Benny shut his eyes and took a breath of his beloved forest air. Night smells of moss and spicy earth drifted enticingly amongst the crowd as crisp, chilly drifts of mist settled for the long wait until dawn.

Benny's nostrils flared and his answer was strangely wistful.

'Who can tell?' he replied. 'All I know is this. When the air smells like almond blossom as the breeze turns the leaves, I will begin my journey, I believe.'

Pud nodded, but he didn't really know what almonds were.

Benny went on. 'The biggest orchards you've ever seen, lie in the Valley of Possibility. The valley surrounds the Tower of Dreams with thousands of almond trees. When they're in bloom, the scent drifts to all the corners of our world. That scent is what I'm waiting for as it will guide me in the right direction. Once I know which way to go, well, that's when I will leave the forest and begin my journey.'

Pud yipped. 'What are almonds, please?'

Benny grinned. 'Nuts, they're a kind of nut.'

Pud nodded and decided he'd like to eat some one day.

Rielle was touched. Timidly, she turned worried eyes to Benny.

'You'd do all that for me?' she asked. 'But, why? It sounds like Wish is a dangerous place. If it is, I don't want you to go. What if you don't return? How could I ever live with myself if something should happen to you?'

Benny smiled and shook his head, sending his curly mane from place to place. Then with lively assurance, he stated, 'I'll return, Rielle, because unicorns always do!'

'But, go all that way, just because I'm sad?' Rielle insisted.

Benny peered at Rielle then looked away. He gazed wistfully at a pocket of stars. 'Just because you're sad, you say?' Sighing, he spoke in a cheerless hush. 'To be sad is to crush the heart of Nature.'

For moments Benny stayed quiet. Then he stared Rielle firmly in the eye and stated with a cheery cry, 'If Hope tells me you have a dream, I promise I'll return with it Rielle, safe and in one piece, to you!'

The herd began to mutter and whisper, nodding their heads and pawing the ground, then they silenced as Coraggio and Candela stepped forward and Candela whickered for all to hear.

'Benny, my dear,' she began, 'a journey can be a peculiar thing and we wouldn't have you go on your own. You will need friends. One friend for high places who can ride swift winds, and one friend for low places, like hidden dens.'

Coraggio then spoke in his deep, careful voice, picking his words with deliberate thought. He nodded at the great grey owls sitting upon the bank close by. They nodded back.

'Hoot, the owl,' he politely asked, 'your chicks can now fly and feed themselves, so your clever wife should manage them well. This journey may last for a year or a night so I don't ask this lightly of you. Will you travel with Benny for the eyes of night and wings of flight, and for all things just and wise?'

The larger of the great grey owls turned his head, opened his eyes wide and after a moment's thought he calmly replied.

'I should think it an honour, great Coraggio. It is done, you can count on me.'

Creatures rustled in the night. It seemed that their meeting had drawn quite a crowd.

Then Candela called out. 'Bibs, are you there? I thought I saw you before. Are you here tonight?'

Rielle wondered who Candela was calling, and at first, all she heard was a scraping, scratchy sort of voice muttering and mumbling from behind some rocks. Then she heard a soft thud and plop, and to her amazement a huge brown snail weaved his way right up to Candela's hooves.

'I'm here, I'm here!' he cheerily called. 'I was just sitting around; you know how it is. I wasn't snooping, you know! Oh no! But there was something doing under the mossy bank, I thought, and so a fellow checks these things out.' The snail's antennae wiggled and weaved as the moon shone a reflection of light onto his shell.

Now this was new and strange! Surely Candela wasn't planning for a snail to go with Benny on his journey? Rielle knew that unicorns were shrewd and smart, so she was unwilling to question judgement much older and wiser than her own, but what in blazes would a snail be good for? Rielle just had to ask.

'Pardon me,' she interrupted, 'I don't want to seem silly or dumb, but how can a snail go?' She stammered. 'I... I mean, how will he keep up? After all, snails are awfully slow, and I know for a fact that Benny's fast.'

The snail turned and stared suspiciously at her. He drew the line at being judged by someone he'd never met! He slid over to Rielle. Crossly, he looked up. He was quite an oozy chap, Rielle decided, but he had sweet brown eyes with large hooded lids and in truth, his face seemed very nice.

'Young lady,' he began abruptly, 'do you think a unicorn, one so brave and bright, would send an *ordinary* snail on a journey, with her child, through the perils of the night?'

Rielle opened her mouth to reply, but Bibs continued.

'A journey of enormous importance such as this requires wits, and extraordinary sense!' He opened his eyes wide, sniffed, and announced with pride: 'In fact, I'm an *Imperial Guard Snail*, a rare and disappearing breed, and while we aren't exactly fast, we aren't exactly slow, so keeping up with Benny should not be a problem in my esteemed opinion.'

Before Rielle had a chance to answer or even gather her thoughts, a new voice spoke from the dark.

'Blah, blah, blah. A hoohey and a phooey! You're such a phoney, Bibs!' Then in quite another tone, full of sugary respect, it addressed the unicorns.

'Candela, what were you thinking? Pardon me, I mean, I know you're wise and gracious and all that, but you know Bibs is daft and fey, that he likes to play and has no sense of the time of day!'

Rielle looked around and sure enough, another snail, just as big but browner, slid quietly by. He had a darker head, wider eyes and the moonlight guided him in a spotlight of his own.

Placing himself squarely at Candela's feet, he looked up and she leaned down so they almost touched, nose to nose. Candela nudged the old snail with delicate affection.

'Dear Bobs, how are you, then? I thought with your great age that you would be fast asleep by now.'

Promptly, Bibs turned away from Rielle and slid to Candela's feet.

'I take offence!' he squeaked, horrified that his character was in question. 'I am not daft or fey! When I was younger I occasionally forgot, but I'm mature now and I know better ways. I remember everything. I'm almost sure I do.'

Rielle was impressed. He certainly was not too slow. In all her life she had no idea such clever snails did exist. But then if unicorns were real, it meant anything was possible after all.

Bobs however, was not to be outdone. Tilting his head with self-importance, he turned again to the unicorns.

'You know, Candela, if you're choosing a guardian for hidden places on the forest floor, I think that Benny will need *me*.' He beamed smugly. 'For this journey he'll need my brains and my knowledge. After all I know my way about in every dell and dale and I've already seen the Valley of Possibility, since I once went with you.'

Candela nodded and her long mane swelled like an ocean current.

'Ah Bobs, it is true, you did once go to the valley with me, and I was grateful for your guardianship at the time. It's true that you know the way, and it's true that you are the master of the small dark places.' She paused, carefully weighing her decision.

'Very well then.' Candela smiled. 'You may go with Benny despite your great age, but only if you promise to guide with wisdom and to take great care.' She nudged old Bobs again. 'Bless you for the offer, my friend.'

'Hang on, hang on, you asked me first,' squawked Bibs. 'Now you're changing your mind and giving me the heave-ho?'

With a sigh, Candela looked closely at both of them. 'Of course not, Bibs, I'd do no such thing.' She and Coraggio exchanged a glance.

'At first Coraggio and I thought to send two friends with Benny but now it seems only right that he should go with three. So, Bibs and Bobs, if you still choose, you may both go for the low, dark places and honourable Hoot will go for the high.'

A gasp of horror went up from the snails. They turned and looked at each other in disbelief.

'Both of us!' exclaimed Bobs. 'Candela, that's impossible. You know Imperial Guard snails steer clear of their relatives if they can!'

Disgusted, Bobs turned his head and sulked, and Bibs pulled a face.

Coraggio stepped forward and if a unicorn can frown, he did. He sniffed the haughty snails with a huff of serious distaste then snorted loudly from his large distended nostrils, sending both snails rolling and falling and tumbling on the ground. He waited, saying nothing.

Eventually, with their usual fuss, Bibs and Bobs righted themselves in a messy, greasy kind of way and turned back, at last, to the unicorns. Seeing the expression on Coraggio's face, though, they hung their heads in shame.

Coraggio waited patiently, and then spoke with deep intent. No one there misunderstood the importance of his words.

'Now I'll say this once and only once, my little slippery friends. Benny is going to the Tower of Dreams to seek the answer to a puzzle. His journey will take him through the treacherous Wish, so this is not a game, and this is not some idle play, for Benny is seeking Hope.' He paused and stared at the snails, and his hot glare made them wilt.

'So,' he continued, 'when you go with him and our wise friend Hoot, we,' he gestured toward the herd, 'will expect great things of you! Be on your guard, be brave, be sharp, but above all else, no matter what, make sure that you honour this important task.' He held their gaze. 'Do you understand?'

Coraggio was huge and bold and although a unicorn, which made him kind and fair, in this frame of mind who would cross his path?

'Yes Coraggio,' Bobs quickly answered, 'I will make a pledge. No matter what a fool Bibs is, I will honour this task and hold it dear above all else!'

Coraggio sighed in despair and then waited for Bibs' reply.

'Of course Coraggio, of course,' Bibs squeaked, 'I know what it is I have to do, so I'm doing this for Benny and, well, naturally, for you!'

Bibs snuck a peek at Bobs at the very moment that Bobs snuck a peek at him. Quick as quick they looked away and pretended that they were the only snail there.

Candela stepped forward again.

'Dearest friends,' she trilled, 'we know you'll do your best. We, the herd, bless you from our hearts. There comes a time when each unicorn must fulfil a destiny and truth, so we're very proud of Benny and his choice of task.' She paused and beamed. 'We send with you on your journey our consent, our thoughts and our greatest love. But above all else, we send with you the power of the herd.'

Coraggio snorted softly. 'Take great care. We wish you a bright and well-lit road, fair weather, and no lack of shelter or of food.'

Candela nodded at the gathering. 'The task is set now; there is no turning back. All that remains is to begin the journey when the time is right.'

She turned and looked adoringly at Benny. 'Benny dear, when you see Hope, be sure to give my love.'

Then like a roll of mist, noiseless and swift, the herd waltzed off to a unicorn's night and the owls, too, turned to other things and sprang away in flight.

In opposite directions the snails hastily retreated to where it is that snails go, and so, in fleeting moments, the glen was quiet, but Benny hadn't moved.

Rielle was astonished. The meeting was over and everything was decided, just as quickly as that! How could it be that such important decisions and plans were made so swiftly?

This was the biggest day that Rielle could remember in the longest time. So much had happened since the morning. First, waking up inside the tree, then her hat blowing away, and then meeting Benny and a unicorn herd, not to mention other creatures she'd never seen before. She felt such affection for Benny. He was planning a wild, unknown journey just for her!

In a sudden show of gratitude, Rielle hugged Benny with all her strength. Against his silky white neck, she could feel the beating of his heart.

'You're wonderful, Benny,' she whispered into his curly mane. 'I've never had a unicorn friend.' Shyly, she stood again.

Benny grinned and his huge green eyes shone brightly.

Pud understood that they'd found a new best friend and he grinned happily from ear to ear.

'When are you going, Benny?' Pud asked.

Benny sensed the call of night and knew he'd done with chatting for now.

'I'll let you know,' he replied quickly. 'Goodnight!'

With a high flung buck of glee, Benny the little unicorn galloped out of sight to where the herd had gone to bed, to doze in peace and dream that night.

Rielle couldn't keep her eyes open anymore. Weary beyond belief, she and Pud lay down in their little den. Knowing they were safe, they soon fell sound asleep.

For the briefest moment, the mild air turned crisp and chill, and a hard breeze shifted moodily about, as trees bent their branches this way, then that, and leaves with endings fluttered to the ground. Like a blessed relief, slumber entwined the forest, gathering the trees, and the stones and moss, into a pattern of woven beauty that was occasionally exposed by the blazing moon.

CHAPTER 4

Wish for a dream and make it come true

Above the tree-top tips, the moon still swayed, fit and full of running. Wafting on the breeze, there rode a scent so delicate and sweet that the gentle deer stopped to sniff. It was the scent of almond blossoms.

Amongst the dozing herd, Benny stirred and sniffed the air. He knew there'd be no rest or slumber for him that night as the scent of almonds beckoned, and it was time to leave!

Going from the herd, who blessed him as he passed, Benny the little unicorn stepped quietly into the moonlit dale and summoned first Hoot, then Bibs and Bobs, with a small high sound that Pud heard in his sleep, causing him to softly bark, but buried deep in dreaming, he did not awake. Rielle slept on unaware, in deepest slumber, and did not stir.

So soon, secretly and unannounced, the journey had begun.

In the calm and quiet of night's embrace, Benny, Hoot, Bibs and Bobs met by a tinkling waterfall. Benny dipped his horn into the stream, which made the water bubble wildly, then cleansed, it trickled on. Benny chuckled. He loved to play with water. Suddenly serious, Benny looked at the gathered company.

'Dear friends,' he whispered, in keeping with the night, 'I have never been on a big adventure before. I think I know what our next move is, but something tells me that teamwork is best. So, before we begin, let's make a council and then decide which steps to take.' He turned to the great grey owl.

'Wise Hoot, I feel that our path should turn right after this brook. What are your thoughts? Do we go right, or is the breeze tinkering with us?'

Promptly, Hoot flew to the highest tree-top and sat in deliberate thought. Then, flying from mighty topmost branch of tree to tree, at last he knew what to say. With killing speed he dove back to the forest floor, stopping short with lightning brakes to perch upon the rock he'd been sitting on before.

'Young Benny, I agree. The breeze whispers that a sharp turn right should take us to the Valley of Possibility.' Then, never one to talk too much, Hoot hooded his large white eyes and sat.

Benny turned to Bibs and Bobs. The snails reached his knees. Looking the older snail squarely in the eye, Benny began again.

'Bobs, which direction should we take, from your viewpoint on the forest floor?'

Now Bobs the old guard snail took nothing with a pinch of salt. For him each and every thing in life was solemn, stern, and measured with care and thought.

Snap decisions and minds made up in haste were not for him, but Bobs had been to Wish before, so this journey wasn't new. With a definite voice and no debate, he stated clearly, 'We go right!'

Then, before Benny had a chance to think, Bibs piped up loud and shrill.

'What about me? I hope even though I'm the youngest of this crew that I have a right to speak up too?'

In a whisper, Benny cautioned. 'Shush, settle and be still, or you'll wake our sleeping guests.'

Bibs looked confused. 'But I thought they were coming on this journey. I mean, aren't we going because of them?'

'No, I mean yes,' countered Benny. He sighed. 'No, they aren't coming with us. Yes, we are going for Rielle. I want you to understand that even though we're seeking Hope, if Rielle comes with us, being human, the chances are that she will get in the way. So, she needs to stay in the forest, while we find Hope for her instead.'

'Um... ' began Bibs, but he was quickly silenced by a look of scorn from Bobs.

Benny nudged Bibs gently with his nose. 'Of course I'm going to ask you too, but you'll have to learn to be patient and wait.' Then feeling sorry for the younger snail, Benny spoke in a kinder tone. 'Now, in your opinion, young guard snail, which way should we go?'

Although usually hasty, Bibs bowed his head and tried his best to show that he, too, was smart.

'Well, the moon is sitting high above,' Bibs whispered, 'and the night is very young.' He sniffed the air and pointed an antenna like a finger. 'The breeze is carrying a scent of almond blossoms and it's coming from there!' Fast as fast he turned his head and sure enough, he was looking past the tinkling brook and to the right.

'Excellent, then, we all agree,' announced Benny. 'All that remains now, fellows, is to make a plan.'

Bobs cleared his throat loudly, making it obvious he'd like to speak.

'We will need to find the wishing pond,' he began. He paused dramatically and then continued in his most important voice. 'The wishing pond is surrounded by giant moonbeams.' He coughed and cleared his throat. 'It also has a gatekeeper. We must inform the gatekeeper that we are on our way to Wish.' He peered at Benny and Hoot, while haughtily pretending that Bibs wasn't there.

Benny nodded him on.

'But, first of all,' Bobs continued, 'we must be very careful to stay on the track, otherwise we risk going around in circles and never leaving the forest at all.' He paused. All eyes were on him and he made the moment last. 'Are there any questions?' He looked around as if speaking to a crowd of thousands, but Hoot and Benny simply nodded. Bibs didn't query, which was just as well.

'Thank you Bobs,' Benny politely replied. 'Very well, one and all,' he hastened, 'with no further ado, we turn right!'

With furtive steps, utmost quiet and eager strides the crew left the moonlit clearing and disappeared from watching eyes. Hoot flew low and silently, deep in owlish thought. For him this was a journey of great responsibility, so he was determined never to let the others out of sight.

Benny walked slowly at first. He had no intention of getting lost on such an important night. Leading his willing little band, he trod beyond the waterfall and turned sharp right onto a rocky path. Sniffing the air for almond blossoms, he looked up to check on Hoot. Satisfied, he picked up speed. Dense trees and undergrowth hid the moon, so like ghostly shadows, the travellers shifted eerily from place to place. A turn in the path took them uphill where Bobs showed rare excitement.

'We're getting close!' he whispered.

Benny went from walking, to a speedy trot.

Now, the snails, both of them, began to show their stuff. They slid faster with easy style and grace, watching each other warily from the corners of their eyes, and without a single word they began a little race. Not to be outdone, each one paced the other, so that Hoot, from up above, noticed first one snail in the lead, then shortly after, another.

With flaring nostrils and tail high, ears pointed and watchful eyes, Benny climbed the hill without a word, busily looking for the wishing pond.

Then it happened, so suddenly that even Benny faltered.

'What are you seeking?' boomed a deliciously gigantic voice.

The band of friends paused, peering into the night. The forest loomed dark and motionless.

Then, as if by moonbeam magic and scrolling toward them like a festive parcel, a large, mist-covered pond lay before them. A delicate haze twirled over it in tendrils of soft transparent white that seemed to beckon the four.

Like curtains parting, the mists gave way, delighting the friends with what they saw. Giant water lilies grew in the pond, some twice as big as Benny. There were pink and yellow ones with pointy tips and orange and purple ones, all surrounded by enormous leaves that made a kind of path across the water's depths. Reeds swayed and nodded as moonlight shone as brightly as day. The water of the pond lay without a ripple in clear dark blue that reflected images perfectly, like a mirror on a wall. With tiptoe tread the friends crept to the pond's edge, and looking in, there they were!

The snails admired themselves, turning this way then that, as if there were nothing much else to do. Hoot sighed and frowned at them. Benny had more important things to think about as he promptly looked around.

'Hello?' Benny queried softly. 'Are you there?'

No one answered. The owner of the voice was not to be seen.

'Psst!' Hoot scowled at the snails. 'Give your attention here!'

Embarrassed, and jolted from their preening, the snails stood to attention, ignoring each other, of course.

'Bobs,' Benny asked, 'is this the wishing pond?'

Bobs puffed himself to a grander size. 'Well,' he muttered, 'it has been quite some time since I was here I hope you understand, and my old eyes aren't what they used to be.'

Bibs sneered but Hoot nudged him to hold his thoughts.

'Mmm, yes,' continued Bobs, 'in my professional opinion,' he said, glaring hotly at Bibs who was sniggering again, 'this is most certainly a wishing pond of sorts.'

Bobs knew full well that this was the wishing pond that they wanted, but he liked the importance it gave him to be asked.

Just then, a small, green, red-eyed frog bounced from grand lily leaf to lily leaf, flashing a bright blue chest and lovely orange hands and feet.

The travellers watched his every move. Perhaps the frog would know who owned the booming voice, or where the gatekeeper was.

With comic leaps and wild, joyous bounds, the gorgeous frog bounced about the pond. His great red eyes with large black pupils had a knowing look, but although he made each leap look easy, he really didn't have much grace. At times, with widespread toes and thrashing arms and legs, he looked comical despite his beauty and big bounce. Occasionally, he nearly missed his mark, and then drops of water flew in the air, where giant moonbeams turned them into pearls.

Finally, the frog landed with decision on a large lily pad, almost in the centre of the pond. He watched the travellers for a moment and then, satisfied, he quickly ate a flying bug.

Benny began to turn away. After all, it was just a little frog. But the frog barked, croaked and cleared his throat. It was the strangest sound any of them had ever heard; it was so loud, in fact, that Benny flinched, the snails cringed and Hoot had to cover his ears.

'I can open the gate to the wishing pond,' the frog roared.

'You?' Benny asked, amazed. Quickly he recovered. 'I

mean I don't want to be impolite, but you seem so small to have such a big voice and, if you don't mind my saying, I never thought a little frog would be the gatekeeper to a wishing pond.'

Bobs stepped forward, glaring-eyed. 'You!' he bellowed. 'You are not the gatekeeper to this pond!'

No sooner had Bobs spoken than suddenly the pond swished and swirled and a large eye rose from the water and gazed at everyone.

Benny stepped back as Hoot took stock.

The eye was soon joined by another, and then both eyes were joined by a nose, and finally a mouth. A tortoise lunged upward, looking at Benny with a kindly expression. With a sprightly swing, the tortoise turned to glare at the frog.

'I see you're still pretending to be me, Rana, whenever you have the chance. Please hop over and go away and find somewhere else to play.' It wasn't a request; it was an order. As if to prove it, he gave a mighty shake.

With a dramatic bound, Rana, the frog, leapt to sit on a leaf in the middle of the pond. He settled there to wait.

'Oh very well,' sighed the tortoise, 'you may watch. But behave yourself and don't go shouting all over the place. It can be off-putting, you know.'

Turning with good humour, he looked at Benny and his friends.

'Well, well, well, what have we here? It looks like a small white unicorn, two Imperial Guard Snails and a largish noble owl,' the tortoise murmured cheerfully. 'Hmm, let me see, I remember a unicorn, also snowy white, with the longest mane and tail. And well, the last time I saw an Imperial Guard was a long, long time ago; so long ago that I thought there weren't any left out there. And owls, well, owls come by here all the time.'

He paused, then blustered. 'The lovely unicorn - what was her name? Lalacan? No. Canla? No. Delalala? Candlelala or something,' he rumbled on.

Despite the fact that it was obvious the gatekeeper was talking to himself, Benny felt it was time to let him know who they were.

'Candela,' he interrupted in a polite voice. 'Her name is Candela and she is my mother.'

With the most direct gaze and great good humour, the reptile peered at Benny and looked him courteously up and down.

'Hm. Ah, of course. Candela, for the light of candles in the dark! Hmm, let me see, I believe she was in uni-foal and very, very beautiful, filled with graciousness and light.'

Benny waited with his head held high, not sure yet how to reply.

'I have it! Of course! Benemerito... named for great merit and good deeds. She mentioned that would be your name.' The tortoise peered cheerily at Benny. 'Ahhhh, so you must be her little boy!'

Benny blushed and hung his head, not daring to look at Hoot or the snails.

'Well, no one really calls me that, you know. It's really too long for a name, so please, just call me Benny.' He looked up shyly, but at the thought of his mother finding him a name, he was filled with modest pride.

'Benny?' The tortoise savoured the shortened name. 'Ben...nee. Yes, I see. It would be much easier to *say* Benny this and Benny that, but a shame, for it hides the merit and great deeds. But, hmm, maybe not.' He watched Benny shrewdly from practised eyes. 'Maybe... it's wiser if others *see* the deeds and merit, after all.'

It was now clear to the travellers that the gatekeeper liked to think out loud.

Still peering at Benny, another quick smile crossed the gatekeeper's large cheerful face. 'Well met then, Benny unicorn,' he greeted, in a kind yet commanding way.

Benny bowed deep and low. This was a great moment indeed! He never imagined he would meet the keeper of a wishing pond.

'Thank you,' he respectfully replied. 'I am honoured, Sir, to make your acquaintance. It was very good of you to greet us here, and now, please let me introduce my friends. This is Hoot for the eyes of night and the wings of flight and for all things just and wise, and this is Bibs and this is Bobs, who've come to help me with hidden places on the forest floor.'

The gatekeeper dipped his head, acknowledging them. Then, with a noble air and a gentlemanly manner, he formally introduced himself.

'As you may understand,' he stated, his eyes thoughtful, 'I watch the gate to another land. Well, Wish to be exact! My name is Oobaat, and my everlasting duty is to attend this task. As you may or may not know, the land of Wish is not a place to take lightly, my friends.'

Oobaat shook his head. 'Ahh,' he muttered, 'many venture here to this gate, wishing this and wishing that and although I guard the gate, I have no power to stop their wishes, give advice, or change their thoughts in any way. That is not my place. All I do is record their presence, reason for going, the time and the date.' The gatekeeper sighed. 'Goodness knows what happens with all those wishes.' Drawing the others into his confidence, he spoke in hushed tones. 'Some strange characters come by here, you know, and I often wonder what becomes of their wishes. It makes me shudder to think!'

Benny and the others nodded.

Oobaat's eyes became piercing then, and for a moment his pleasant manner and voice changed. 'As you may or may not know, wishing is a tempting thing, quite a delicate business really, when you think about it hard and long.'

Rana began to croak and leap as if he knew what was coming next and although he'd heard it all before, the excitement of knowing was too much to take.

Oobaat puffed his cheeks out and called aloud:

I wish I fat
I wish I thin
I wish I rich
I wish I quick
I wish I climb
I wish I fly
I wish I tall
I wish I small

I wish for boat
I wish for moat
I wish for gold
I wish for jewels
I wish for socks and for shoes
Make my wishes all come true
Give me jam for dog and cat
No, make that cream so they get fat!

Oobaat stopped and blinked at the three friends. 'Sounds ridiculous, doesn't it?' he quipped. 'Well, those are the clever ones, if you want to know!'

The gatekeeper glared at Rana, who was leaping about and making far too many loud noises. Rana took the hint and pretended that it was his idea to sit still again.

'I have seen many wishes go astray,' continued Oobaat. 'Oh, they often start out quite well and lull wishers into thinking they're clever, but I'm the one who sits here aeon in and aeon out, as wishes fall and tumble down.' He looked directly at Benny. 'Do you understand that making a wish is not the same as having a dream?'

Benny nodded. Of course he understood. Wishing wasn't a unicorn thing. Unicorns had everything they wanted, right inside their hearts and heads.

The travellers could now see that Oobaat, though cheery, also carried a deep burden as gatekeeper and that it could make him thoughtful and sad.

The tortoise opened his eyes a little wider. 'You see, young Benny, a wish usually comes from your mind but a dream is a truth from your heart. The easiest way to know the difference is what you get from it in the end. Do you know what I mean?'

Benny nodded again. Of course he did. Unicorns knew these things!

Satisfied, Oobaat began to chant in a magnificent and daunting voice:

'It is clearly stated, in lore, that one must be very careful what is wished for. One must be clever and think it through, for if it comes from the mind and not from the heart, then it isn't the right thing for you!'

He was so commanding that Bibs and Bobs hid in their shells.

However, despite his hiding, Bibs was confused. He wasn't sure if he understood what the tortoise meant. *If you want something*, Bibs wondered to himself, *you just want it, don't you?* What difference did it make where you wanted it from? All this talk of hearts and minds, wishing and dreaming, surely it made life too complicated. Then Bibs stopped thinking and listened again.

'Please don't misunderstand,' Oobaat continued in a gentler way as he noticed the snails hiding. 'Dreams can be great and wondrous things!'

Then Oobaat seemed to grow. With glaring eyes he looked fully at Benny.

'It is my duty now,' he rumbled, 'as gatekeeper to this wishing pond, to record what your task might be within the land of Wish.' So powerful was he that even wise Hoot quivered.

But Benny had only one answer. Proudly, from his place of truth, Benny very clearly stated, 'I am seeking

Hope.'

Oobaat's eyes popped in complete amazement and his mouth formed an 'o.' He frowned. 'Hope, hmm? What's this then, a unicorn seeking Hope? Has the outside world come to an end, and I wasn't yet informed?'

Benny quickly shook his head. 'Oh no Sir, it's not for me! You see, I need to find Hope for a friend. My friend is lost and sad and frightened, and she believes she has no dreams. She might not be able to find Hope for herself and so we're going to the Valley of Possibility. Somewhere in the valley is the Tower of Dreams. That's where Hope lives. I need to ask Hope for an answer to a puzzle.'

Oobaat opened his eyes wider still and raised his cheery chin.

'Well, well,' he chuckled, approval clear in his eyes. 'How could I dislike such a noble cause? Truly, young unicorn, this is a gracious deed. Your mother named you well!'

Then, before anyone could speak again, Rana jumped up and down with a boom and raucous shout. 'So can I open the gates now, huh?' With his red eyes watching and alert, he perched with every muscle in his body as keen as mustard to perform the task.

But Oobaat was not to be hurried or interrupted and with exaggerated patience he turned to the frog. Oozing tolerance, he looked doubtfully at him.

'Because you're still quite young and shall we say, er, a little silly, I'll overlook your rudeness and unnecessary interruption. I haven't finished speaking yet, but when I do, if I feel it's right, then I'll say yes and bid you open the gates for the guests and I.'

Rana didn't look a bit anxious at being scolded. Instead, with a huge wide grin he sat stony still. Waiting, he did as he was told.

With a last warning look at Rana and finality in his voice, Oobaat turned back to Benny. 'Now where was I in my train of thought? Oh yes, I remember now! Young Benny, your task is worthy and truly gracious so I personally approve, and because of that I will help you pass and take you the easy way through. It is with great tribute that in my role of gatekeeper I offer you safe passage, wish you luck and all the very best.'

Then Oobaat swam right up to the bank and with a great deal of shuffling, shunting, water flying and lots of grunting, he turned and looked at the travellers. 'Hop on my back,' he called, 'and I'll give you a ride!'

Treading carefully, Benny walked onto the tortoise's back. Following on, with a slip and slide, trailed a timid Bibs and Bobs. They were all amazed at how they managed to fit.

Reassuring them, Oobaat cautioned. 'Stay very still and all will be well. You wouldn't do this with any other tortoise, but don't be alarmed, as this is my job. Now listen carefully, for I will tell you this. No matter what happens you must have faith, and if you feel you want to fret, I ask you to be strong, be true, believe and trust, be brave and never doubt!'

With eager eyes and legs splayed wide, Benny found his balance. The snails slid and slipped but soon found that if they leaned on Benny, they were fine. Hoot flew up then fluttered down to perch calmly on Benny's back.

As soon as they were settled, Oobaat slid off the bank and, paddling swiftly, carried the travellers without a hitch. Half-way across the pond he suddenly stopped, which almost sent Benny flying and made the snails seasick, but Hoot stayed with perfect balance on top of Benny's back.

'Rana, if you would be so kind,' Oobaat called, 'you can open the gates for us now!'

With leaps of multicoloured joy and booming raucous calls, the frog made a fantastic leap. With a lack of grace but perfect aim he landed with his usual drama right in the centre of a large purple flower. The lily slowly began to move and as it did so, Rana leapt away. The travellers stared as the flower's centre opened.

Oobaat hollered. 'Hold on tight, here we go!'

Almost before they had time to think, the tortoise dove down deep, right through the centre of the purple water lily.

Now water is water so it makes good sense to wonder how, if they were under water, they might exist, but through that void there was another world, another time and another place. In some way that not even Benny could explain, they all remained upon Oobaat's back, well balanced and truly safe.

The tortoise swam with powerful strokes through clear sweet waters of palest blue, and still on his back, the others held their breath and remembered his words: *trust, have faith, be true.*

The clear liquid passed through Benny's mane and tail, making them stream behind him like giant fins and tails of fish, but Hoot's feathers lay limp and soggy; the owl wasn't used to this. Bibs and Bobs were used to wet and slippery things, but swimming wasn't one of them, so in a truly sensible way, they shut their eyes and didn't look!

Benny held on with mounting excitement and saw in his mind that other land, the Tower of Dreams and Hope.

For a short time, it's true, they were soggy, but soon, so soon that they were all amazed, they reached the other shore! With a well-timed leap, Oobaat landed nimbly on a sandy place.

With jelly legs, Benny leapt off the tortoise's back, and the snails let go their suction with a loud pop, landing wrong side up with a squishy splat.

Hoot's wings and feathers were wet and heavy, so with as much dignity as he could find, he quietly waddled on behind until with a great shudder and shake, he made water fly in all directions and soon his feathers were, well, nearly right.

Swiftly, Oobaat checked that they were fine. 'Until next time!' he called. Then with mighty strokes, he dove deeply and was gone.

Silence grasped the travellers as they turned to look at Wish. The light was neither night nor day and the air was pleasant and warm. But the travellers found that their mood was sober and quietly grave. It was true that they were in Wish, but the journey had only just begun.

CHAPTER 5

Impish frog or wicked me

The deep of night still flayed the forest when Rielle suddenly awoke. She sighed with satisfaction. She was in a bewitching haven with enchanting creatures. *She belonged.* Feeling protected, she snuggled under her cloak where it was pleasantly warm, while somewhere close, Pud contentedly snored. Rielle knew that all was well.

She took several deep, long breaths and wondered what the perfume in the air could be. Her eyelids closed and her breathing deepened as sleep stretched out its persistent hand. Gentle dozing became her friend, as rest quietly called her name. Rielle began to drift with sleep, but she had been mistress of her fate for too long, so suspicion was a friendly habit, which is why her mind battled and woke her up.

'That scent!' She bolted upright. 'That scent was not there at all during the day,' she muttered, 'and it isn't woodsy or forest-like, which makes it something new.' She shook poor Pud who was happily snoring, forcing him to wake with a wary bark.

'Pud, Pud,' Rielle whispered frantically, 'can you

smell that? It's delicious and sweet and I'll bet anything you want that it's the smell of almond blossoms!'

Pud peered at her through the dim glow of night, his expression a mix of slumber and growing suspicion.

'Don't you see?' Rielle went on. 'If that's the scent of almond blossom, then we have to let Benny know!'

Pud knew that when his mistress had hold of an idea there would be no more rest, so he began to stretch, yawn and shake.

'No time for that or we'll lose half the night,' Rielle snapped. 'Come on Pud, let's get going!' She pulled her boots on and grabbed her cloak, but Pud was making the best of things, so he finished stretching anyway.

As Rielle stepped from their little den, she gazed at a transformed world. Mystically capturing the woven night in its beams of spinning fairy floss, the moon still shone. But it sat lower and was trickier than the sun, so bright moonbeams stretched into the forest where sunlight would never go. Rielle almost forgot her new mission, preferring to sit and look at the night's charm, but she forced herself on.

'We need the herd,' she whispered to Pud. 'If Benny's anywhere, he'll be there.'

Pud sniffed the air then trotted off to find the unicorns. Rielle glanced around then quickly followed. Sensible Pud found unicorn tracks and then saw the unicorn glow, so he led Rielle with perfect ease to the quietly dozing herd.

In a pocket of moss-strewn forest, so old that it made the stars seem young, the unicorns flamed in white gentle glory, basking in a light of their own special power that blazed like a brilliant meteor.

Rielle was overcome. Unicorns in sleep were more majestic than it was possible to believe! As usual, they were completely daunting and words were already sticking in her throat. She hated to disturb them as they seemed so content, but they saw her before she saw them.

Straight away, Candela understood. She sighed inwardly at the brave human girl, and knew that now, there could be trouble to face. Candela knew humans better than they knew themselves. Despite her misgivings, she did what unicorns do. With a gentle manner she glided over to meet Rielle.

Candela bowed graciously. 'Rielle?' Then effortlessly, she shifted her light to surround the girl and the dog.

Rielle braced herself. She was sure it would be cold but instead she was agreeably surprised. The glowing light was warm and friendly and harvested her heart onto friendly shores. Pud shivered with delicious joy as the light tickled his coat and made him sneeze. Pud wasn't silly; he knew this was a treat, so in true dog fashion he made the most of each moment and greedily lay down and rolled blissfully on the grass. The glow's warmth calmed Rielle, as Candela had intended. Rielle almost wondered why she'd been so frantic and rushed.

'Rielle?' Candela asked again, as she pinned the girl with enquiring eyes.

'Um,' Rielle began, 'I know I should be sleeping but I just woke up for a moment, and it was then I noticed that the air smells nice.' As soon as she said it out loud she knew it sounded silly. *Who would wake up and dash across the forest just to let someone know that the air smells nice?*

Candela nodded once.

'I thought it might be the smell of almond blossom,' Rielle stammered, as she floundered in the depths of Candela's waiting eyes. 'I thought... I just thought that maybe if the scent in the forest right now was almonds, well, I thought that Benny, in case he hadn't noticed, might like to know.'

'Ah,' smiled Candela, 'thank you, Rielle.' She paused and felt sorrow ride her heart as she watched the girl battle with uncertain thoughts. Candela knew that honesty was the only way, so she didn't hesitate.

'Benny, Hoot, Bibs and Bobs are gone,' she continued, locking Rielle with a steadfast gaze.

'Gone?' Rielle was confused. 'But Benny was waiting for the smell of almond blossoms and now it's here, isn't it? Does that mean he'll be going on the journey to Wish another time? When the scent returns?'

With earnest eyes Pud looked up at Candela. An unspoken message passed between them.

'No, Rielle, they won't be waiting for another time,' Candela answered with resolve. 'They have gone on the journey to Wish for you, on this night.'

Blood rushed to Rielle's face. *They couldn't go to Wish without her!*

'But,' she began, 'they've gone without me! How can they go without me?' Respect for Candela kept her calm, but it wasn't how she wanted to be. 'I needed to go to Wish with them, don't you see? Why did they sneak off?

Why didn't they also take me?'

'Perhaps,' Candela quietly replied, 'they can do what it is that you can't.'

Pud whimpered. Concern for his mistress gripped his heart.

'Come, Rielle,' Candela consoled, 'why don't you let it be? Benny will find the Tower of Dreams and Hope, and you needn't fear that he won't return.'

'But it's my journey too,' Rielle blurted out. 'I need to go to Wish!'

Candela paused before her next reply as Rielle was determined to play with power. Candela sought words of a subtle nature but knew that humans could be difficult to guide.

'Don't you mean the Tower of Dreams, Rielle?' Candela queried. 'Wish isn't what Benny's seeking. Wish is just a place of passing, on the way to his mission for Hope.'

'I, uh, I wanted to go with them,' Rielle muttered. 'I should go, shouldn't I? I mean, this journey is for me.'

'Exactly,' Candela whispered, 'the journey is for you. However, we all felt that due to Wish being what it is, you might have trouble finding Hope yourself.'

Rielle looked at Candela and blinked. 'I thought if I went along I wouldn't be looking by myself. I thought…. ' Rielle looked away. She could no longer bear Candela's gaze.

'It's best, Rielle,' Candela gently prompted, 'if you leave this to Benny and his helpers and that you now take your faithful Pud and return to sleep.' She knew there was something brewing in the girl's heart and was almost sure what it was. 'Go to bed, young Rielle,'

Candela urged gently again. 'All will be well, you'll see.'

Pud looked at Candela and the unspoken message between them was confirmed.

Rielle nodded and tried to smile, but she couldn't face the expression in Candela's eyes. 'Goodnight,' she whispered, and turned back to her den.

Happily, with a face-splitting grin at the thought of more sleep, Pud loped by Rielle's side. Then he did a doggy Spanish walk that expressed his content. He looked around, but to his dismay Rielle wasn't there. Rielle was staring at the moon; the same orange moon that had lit their way the night before, when they had almost fallen to their doom.

Pud became uneasy. It seemed that Candela's unspoken warning might come true. He went back to Rielle and gazed up at her. Making the biggest, saddest eyes that he could, he placed a paw onto her foot and whined. Then, knowing he was beaten, he gave up in defeat.

Rielle knew what it was she wanted and nothing, not even faithful Pud and all his pleading, was going to change that!

'Come on, Pud,' she whispered, 'we're going to find out where Benny has gone.' She began to walk briskly through the forest but Pud stayed put and didn't move.

Watching from a distance, Candela understood. It was obvious that Rielle had a secret plan, but no unicorn could interfere with a human choice. She felt disappointment for the girl.

Coraggio stepped close to Candela's side. 'Remember, my dear,' he soothed, 'that at least she has our mark on her brow.'

Candela nodded and her mane swayed and shook. 'Yes, that was the right decision, but I wonder how long it will take her to discover what it means?'

Then, because there was nothing that they could do, Candela and Coraggio rejoined the dozing herd. They could offer their light and they could offer their warmth, they could offer advice and care, but they drew the line at giving away power, for humans had a free will and a destiny of their own.

Rielle looked around for Pud. He wasn't there. That was unusual, but the last two nights and a day had been altogether unusual, especially when it came to Pud's usual behaviour. She stopped and saw that he hadn't moved.

'Come on, Pud,' she begged. 'Oh please, Pud, don't let me down now.'

It was then that Pud knew he wasn't going to get more sleep. He knew Candela had been afraid of this. He knew he wasn't happy about it, but he also knew that where Rielle led, he had a duty to follow and protect. He raised himself and looked back at the herd, but all he could see was their glorious glow.

Pud sighed. With droopy ears and his tail between his legs, he slunk glumly up to Rielle. She hugged him, and despite himself, his honest heart bounced. How could he leave his sweet, wilful mistress, just because he suspected she was wrong?

'Good boy,' Rielle crooned. 'Now Pud, please pick up Benny's tracks and show me where they've gone tonight!'

Faithful Pud, despite his best intentions, was soon

running with his nose to the ground following a fresh, clean scent.

Behind him, Rielle ran as fast as she could. Knowing that her behaviour was sneaky and thankless, she didn't want the herd to know she was gone. Her heart tugged with guilt, but she quickly put the thought aside. Justifying that this journey was for her after all, she decided that it was right and proper that she should go to Wish, no matter what it took!

Pud ran like a bloodhound with a loose-tongued grin as he found the snail's tracks and dislodged stones. Benny and the others hadn't been long gone as Pud crossed a feather that belonged to Hoot. This was easy - there was nothing to it - but then abruptly, he stopped. Benny's scent and the snail's tracks had vanished!

Rielle caught up. 'What is it Pud? What's going on? Why have you stalled all of a sudden?'

Pud ran around in little circles with his nose to the ground, until baffled, he stopped and looked at her.

'Perhaps they've hidden their tracks on purpose,' Rielle mumbled. 'Come on, Pud, let's try over there.' They ran several paces through the black of night, but suddenly, a blinding light pierced the dark so brightly that they couldn't see a thing.

'Who goes there?' boomed a voice. 'What are you seeking? Tell me now!'

Rielle and Pud froze. Rielle shivered, fearing the worst from the enormous voice. Could this be why the scent was lost? Rielle's first thought was to run back to the herd, but she steadied. Something terrible might have happened to Benny and he might need her help.

The moonbeams paled and Rielle and Pud realised they were standing on the shores of a little lake. Mesmerised, they tiptoed to the water's edge and peered in. Pud raised his hackles at the huge dark dog looking back at him, but then sheepishly realised he was seeing himself, so he nodded politely and turned back to Rielle. She saw her reflection and was reminded of the star-scar on her brow. A pang of nostalgia for the kindness and truth of Candela and Coraggio rushed through Rielle. She fervently hoped that little Benny and the others were unharmed. Determination gripped her.

'It's not your business who I am,' she called back in her grandest voice, 'or even where I'm going. I do ask you a question, though. What have you done with a small white unicorn, two rare guard snails and a great grey owl?' In the brief silence that followed, Rielle noticed that giant lilies were growing in the pond.

'Done? Done?' rumbled the voice. 'Done what with a unicorn, snails and an owl? Done what? Harmed them? They're not here, that's for sure, but I can promise I've done nothing wrong!' Then in a sulky tone, the speaker scolded, 'Oh, and while I think of it, *all* unicorns are white.'

'Then show yourself,' called Rielle. 'If you know where they are and you promise they're not hurt, show yourself, come out and be brave. We need to speak with you before the night becomes old.'

A moment later, a small colourful frog bounced onto a lily leaf in front of her. The frog looked at her and she looked at it, then Pud barked loudly and began wagging his tail.

'Oh it's just a frog, Pud,' Rielle grumbled. 'No need to get too excited.'

Pud, however, barked again.

Just as quickly, the frog roared back. 'Hello!'

Like shying ponies, Rielle and Pud jumped, amazed in the way Benny had been. 'You!' Rielle gawped. 'How does someone your size have a voice like that?'

Rana stared smugly from startling red eyes. 'Just lucky, I guess,' he smirked.

Recovering, Rielle frowned. 'Right, okay. Shall we get down to business then?' She didn't wait for an answer, but carried on. 'This is Pud and I'm Rielle. Can you please tell us if you've seen a little unicorn and his friends?'

Rana was annoyed. The human girl was rude. Her rough manner wasn't what he deserved.

'My name's Rana,' he pouted, 'and maybe I'll tell you, *Ree-elle*, or maybe I won't!' Then, grinning slyly, he turned his back and ignored them both.

Rielle's hackles were up. 'Oh, forget it. I doubt whether you have the first idea about anything! Come on Pud, let's go. This booming-voiced pipsqueak thinks he has power.'

But as Rielle started to move, Rana began to laugh and, unlike his voice, his laughter was soft, and crackled in his throat. Rielle suspected that the frog was being deliberately annoying but despite herself, she stopped in her tracks.

She shrugged. 'Hooley dooley! Okay, I give up! What's funny?'

Rana bounced. 'You! You don't have the first idea, do you?'

Rielle frowned, puzzled. She glared at the wayward creature.

'I have no idea what you're going on about, that's for sure!'

In a fit of triumph, Rana danced from lily pad to lily pad, croaking happily with every landing, as Rielle watched, arms akimbo, annoyance plainly showing on her face. Pud, however, wagged his tail and grinned. He secretly liked the silly frog.

Rana stopped bouncing, suddenly serious. 'This is a wishing pond,' he announced, 'and I can let you in if you like.'

'A wishing pond?' Rielle gasped. *Was that what she hoped it was?*

'They went in,' was Rana's only response.

'They? Do you mean Benny and the others?' Rielle asked, excitement beating on her brow.

Rana nodded. 'I can let you in if you want.'

Sensible caution mingled with Rielle's excitement. How did she know he was speaking the truth? It was a small lake after all. She wasn't just going to leap in blindly so that she and Pud could miserably drown.

'So, if I jump in here,' she began, 'where do I end up?'

'No! No! No!' Rana shook his head and sprang up and down. 'You can't just jump in! That would be no good! I can let you in though, if you want.'

Rielle's excitement changed back to annoyance. 'Let me in to where?' she snapped.

'Where do you want to go?' asked Rana shrewdly.

'Where did the others want to go?'

Rielle's heart bounced. 'Wish!' she breathed. 'Can you get us into Wish?'

Rana jumped a somersault, landed and croaked. 'Yes!'

'How? How do you do it?' Rielle asked breathlessly.

Rana just made an important face.

'Please,' Rielle begged, 'please tell me how I can reach the others.'

'Wait,' Rana frowned, 'there's some stuff you're supposed to hear first.' He shut his eyes and screwed them tight. 'Okay, I think I've got it now.'

Rana opened his eyes and muttered. 'Wishes can be trouble, dreams can be good; the difference is in the end, er, I think.' He pulled a wry face. 'Um, there's more.' He coughed. 'Thoughts often find the wrong doors. If your heart's missing, but you have a mind, you can muck it all up, that's for sure!'

Pud tilted his head in confusion and Rielle couldn't make any sense of Rana's prattle. She and Pud watched and waited.

Rana blinked rapidly. 'There's other stuff, but what the heck, and since I know why you're going, hey, let's get on with it!'

'Not so fast, frog!' Rielle wanted to go but she wasn't blindly following a frog she'd just met. 'How are we getting there? Is it safe? How do I know Benny was really here?'

Rana looked hurt. 'Why would I lie?' he asked. 'What use would that be? But if you want to check the record books, just read what's written on the lily pads.'

Despite none of it making sense, Rielle and Pud tiptoed to the shore and looked at the lily pad to which Rana pointed. Sure enough, the names of Benny, Hoot, and Bibs and Bobs were there, with a time of day and a date.

Rielle looked around at other lily pads, and in the finest spidery writing she'd mistaken for leaf veins, were written the names of thousands of visitors from over a period of many aeons.

'It's how we keep the records straight,' Rana proudly pointed out.

'We?' Rielle looked around. 'Is there someone else here?'

'We, er, I mean, me. It's really all the same thing,' Rana chuckled innocently. 'So, do you believe me now?'

Rielle realised that there'd be no point in all these written names if there wasn't a good reason for them being there, but there was still something that didn't sit right about this flashy little frog. She looked piercingly at him and he grinned widely back as she wondered what it was that she didn't quite trust.

However, the tracks and scents had led to this pond, so Benny and the others had certainly been here. She decided there was only one thing to do. She had to take a chance.

'So,' she faltered, 'how do we get to Wish?'

'Uh, there's other stuff you need to know,' stalled Rana. Then proudly he cried, 'You have to trust, be brave, be true, and dive in quick where I show you!'

'We got that part, but where is it we're going exactly?' hastened Rielle sourly.

Rana paused slyly then pointed with a cheeky grin. 'You're going through the centre of that purple water lily.'

Horrified, Rielle glared at him. 'Dragon's tail! Do you think we're either completely bonkers or utterly desperate? How can that take us anywhere? Obviously, it's just more water through there or the bottom of the lake!'

'Yes,' Rana breathlessly replied, 'but only for a little minute and then before you even know it you will land on the shores of Wish.'

With a steely eye, Rielle glared at him, but curiosity got the better of her.

'What do we do then? Do we swim or what? Explain to me why we simply won't drown?'

Rana made his most truthful face. 'Yes, you can swim if you like but you don't need to. It just takes you there, and you can't drown because no one ever has. But if you're afraid, just hold your breath, you know, in case. You can trust me, Rielle. Why would I lie?'

Rielle pondered for a moment and tried to work out what didn't seem right. She looked at Pud but he didn't know, so she took a deep breath and made up her mind.

'I... I'll have to take your word,' she began, 'but if you lead us astray, I promise you, Rana the frog, that whether I'm dead or alive, I'll haunt you every day, should this just be some evil trick or your wicked sense of humour.'

Rana grinned from ear to ear.

'Oh, all right then, let's go, but remember what I said!' Rielle shouted.

Rana whooped with joy. In one huge colourful leap he flailed onto the purple lily. He shoved the flower through the water until it lay next to the shore.

'When it opens, jump in!' he called.

With outrageous exuberance, he pounced on the flower's centre then he quickly bounced up and away. In a gentle movement of practised slow motion, the lily's centre began to open.

Amazed, Rielle and Pud gawped, but they didn't make moves to jump in.

Rana became worried. They were taking too long to think about it. In truth, he was frightened by his bold bragging and this bold move. Oobaat was due back any moment from escorting the others and if he found out what Rana had done, all hell was bound to break loose. Rana was jittery and so he puffed himself out and made lots of noise, all the time thinking one thing: *What if, what if, what if, the gatekeeper returns?*

'Go,' Rana called, 'go. Don't wait. You have to go now or it will shut!'

Rielle was afraid. She stalled. Was it going to be safe? She stood on the shores in hesitation, trembling and hoping that it wouldn't be awful. Loneliness and fear gripped her uncertain spirit and she put out her hand to touch Pud on the head. Then, in an unswerving moment, she knew that she had to go to Wish, no matter how frightened or worried she was.

She sucked in a deep breath. 'Come on, Pud,' Rielle whispered through grim, tight lips, 'we do it now or never!'

Pud put on his bravest face. He'd secretly been hoping Rielle would change her mind so that they could return to the safety of the forest. He sighed. Failing that, though, he'd keep his word and the silent promise he'd made to Candela. *Through thick or thin, no matter what, he'd guard his mistress through any peril.*

Rielle patted his head. 'When I count to three, Pud,' she tremulously whispered. Pud rolled his eyes and looked at Rana, but the quirky frog was jittering around.

'One, two, three!' called Rielle, but she and Pud didn't move.

Rana roared his calls into the night. 'Hurry, hurry, hurry,' he boomed and barked. 'Hurry, hurry for goodness sake!'

'Okay, this time, Pud.' Rielle kept her hand on Pud's head, and bending her knees, she prepared to leap, sure that this time she would go.

'One, two, three!' she called again, as her upper body shifted but her feet didn't move. Poor Pud began to leap, but seeing that his mistress stayed behind, he scrambled at the air, promptly falling back onto the shore.

'Okay Pud, let's go!' Rielle leapt high and hard.

Quickly, recovering his balance, Pud joined her with a huge bound of his own. Their jump landed them onto the lily where a whoosh of tide came up to greet them. Together, they were swept like so much nothing, into the waiting turquoise vortex.

Rielle and Pud realised that they had no control. The vortex had a mind of its own, tossing them around like straws on a tide, yet it was definitely taking them somewhere. Pud pinned his ears back and gritted his teeth. The vortex was worse than having a bath. The only thing he wanted was a warm, dry place.

'Please take us to Wish,' Rielle begged, as she grabbed Pud and held him tightly. 'Please take us to Wish, and I promise I'll try to always be good.'

Rielle's mind raced, regretting her decision by each moment. *That frog*, she thought with the brilliance of hindsight, *was shifty or nervous, that's what he was.* She swallowed some water as her hair slapped her face. *He knew something and he wasn't letting on.*

Just then, a huge tortoise sped past, coming from the opposite direction. He stared at them and they stared at him.

Oobaat spun around. *A girl and a dog?* He panicked. *How did they get into the vortex?* Alarmed he called out. 'Stop, please stop!'

Even if they'd had some control, it was already too late for Rielle and Pud. The vortex stopped spinning, and in that moment, it spat them out.

They landed on a sandy shore of pale peach sand that rested like a sleeping baby, relaxed and docile in its mother's arms. Quiet waters of gentle aqua lapped curiously at the yielding shores, and tall sleepy trees, brushed by murmuring breezes, tickled each other as they watched the arrivals.

With several mighty sneezes, Pud blew water from his nose as Rielle sat dumbstruck on the sandy shores. Pud coughed, then gagged and spat, then did a jiggle to the left and a jiggle to the right until some of the water came out of his ears. In disgust, he shook as hard as he could, so hard in fact that he tripped over his feet. Grouchy now, he looked over at Rielle, expecting that she'd be as annoyed and uncomfortable, and at least as soaked, as he was.

Rielle was drenched and covered in sand. Her hair was tangled and her clothes awry, but she didn't seem to notice.

'This is it,' she gloated, secret rapture covering her face. 'This must be Wish.' She grinned. 'Look, Pud, we're really here. Can you believe it? It's exactly as I imagined it would be!'

CHAPTER 6

Battle!

On the other side of Wish, Benny and the others looked solemnly around.

'There's something uncanny about this place,' Bobs whispered.

Hoot nodded. 'It's the air,' he murmured. 'It's almost too warm to breathe.'

Bibs yawned. 'Oh, so sleepy,' he drawled.

Bobs also felt sleep sap his bones, but he refused to show weakness in front of Bibs.

Benny knew something wasn't right when even he wobbled at the knees just as the others fell snoring, open-mouthed, on the sand.

'Wake up,' Benny grunted, 'we aren't here to sleep! This is a business trip!'

Hoot woke straight away, but it took insistent nudging to rouse the snails.

'Where are we?' Bibs drawled, unsteadily.

Bobs sneered. 'You'd remember, wouldn't you, if you hadn't nodded off.'

'Nodded off?' scorned Bibs. 'Wait a minute, so did you!'

'Oh? Really?' Bobs crossly replied. 'I most certainly did not! Are you suggesting I was sleeping on the job?'

'Oh no, I'm not suggesting that at all,' Bibs quipped, 'because I know it, so I'm saying it's true. You are an old fuddy-duddy after all, so shouldn't you be at home tucked in bed right now?'

'Oh, fuddy-duddy eh? How would you know what I was doing, if you were sleeping like a baby?'

'Oh alright then,' bellowed Bibs, 'you tell us where we are, you old pot boiler in a shell!'

'Why, you wretched youngster,' roared Bobs, 'I don't answer to you! Oh, and there's one other thing. Even though you're younger and I'm the senior snail, how is it that when anyone says our names, they always say yours first? It's Bibs and Bobs this, and Bibs and Bobs that. No one ever calls it Bobs and Bibs!'

With red faces and popping eyes, the snails stared furiously at each other.

'So what?' Bibs huffed. 'You tried to steal my place on this journey, right from under my nose. Candela chose me, but you had to interfere and now it looks like we're stuck with you!'

Things looked bad. If it wasn't for Hoot clapping his wings, their squabble might have come to blows.

Stamping a hoof, Benny turned to the snails. 'There are serious things afoot! Remember that you are Imperial Guards! Coraggio warned you, but it seems that's not enough. I won't hesitate to send you home if you carry on like this, but heaven help you if I do send you home, and that Coraggio should find out!' Benny tossed his head and peered around in a wistful way. 'I need all my thoughts and heart and mind, if somewhere, in this strange place, we have a chance of finding Hope.'

He turned to the wide-eyed owl. 'Please Hoot, keep the two O's in line, until I get my bearings and understand our travel plans.'

Hoot raised his eyebrows, blinking hard. 'The two O's?' he asked.

'Yes,' Benny murmured, 'they with their *Oh this, Oh that,* competitions and complaining. Perhaps you can help them keep their snail habits in control.'

Despite themselves, the snails looked at each other. Benny's remarks hurt their feelings. They gave all their loyalty to Benny, but being in trouble and disgrace together oddly gave them something in common. After all, they were only doing what was perfectly natural... well, at least for them. *Did this mean they might have to change?*

Benny had raised his head. 'Shh!' he stated. 'I thought so! I can hear it now!' Nodding to Hoot, he trotted off.

Ignoring each other once again, the snails promptly followed.

As they reached dense shrubbery, Benny put his eye to a small gap in the hedge and peeked at something on the other side. With a nod, he urged the others to look.

Unaware of them sat a baby faun. He had tiny cloven hooves on small goat-like legs and the upper body of a normal boy. On his head were two tiny horns and a tuft of goatish beard grew on his sweet face. Holding musical pipes, he played a lilting tune. The tune swayed in the air, resting for a moment before it swished away. As the music left the pipes, it danced with a mind of its own. It skipped through branches and then played with grasses, making them sway.

The music lulled the group, telling tales of peace. Then, before they knew it, the tune found Benny and the snails, making them skip and prance. Even Hoot forgot his wisdom and age and swooped like a careless young bird.

Enchantingly, the music sent shafts of colour through the air with curly flags of brightest blue. It swerved and danced, making new colours of yellow, orange and purple, too. Forging his way through the wall of music, Benny went to meet the faun.

The faun looked shyly up at him from under black, long-lashed eyes. Promptly, the music stopped. Trees let out a listless sigh as the grass turned yellow. Leaves on trees lost their shiny juicy look, and the once warm air began turning cool.

'Please don't stop,' Benny begged. 'I just wanted to say hello.'

Smiling bashfully and with a nod, the faun began to play again. Promptly, the grass turned green, leaves looked lively and the warm silky air returned.

With a dancing bow, Benny paid his respects. Escorted by a troupe of notes, the friends danced right out of there. Soon they were far away and the spell began to fade.

Bibs was curious. 'Who was that piping in the glade?' he asked Benny.

Benny just smiled. 'You'll see,' was all he replied.

Never one to give up, Bibs slid to Hoot. 'Who was that piping in the glade?'

'You'll see,' Hoot replied, with a cheerful grin.

Bibs frowned. This wasn't fun. No one was telling him anything. Although he hated asking Bobs, he matched his stride to the older snail.

'Who was that piping in the glade, please?'

'You'll see!' Bobs grunted with a superior toss of his head.

Bibs stopped and bellowed. 'Why won't you tell me?' No one answered as they continued up the path. 'Why won't they tell me?' Bibs grumbled. 'If I knew something, I'd tell them.' Feeling snubbed, he yelled out. 'I'm not silly just because I'm the youngest!' But the others were getting farther away. 'If I have to watch and listen at every turn we take,' Bibs grunted, 'I'm going to find out who that piper in the glade is, one day.' Making a dash for it, he caught up with the others.

And so the travellers continued on. They moved briskly through a lush forest of tall saplings that rustled in the friendly breeze. Things were going smoothly, as the memory of the piping faun gave them tunes to hum. Benny was in the lead with careful Hoot above and the snails by his sides. Birds trilled and the scent of almond blossom wafted, rich with messages from the Valley of Possibility.

Unexpectedly, a sharp stab flickered through Benny's forehead. He slowed his steps, bobbed his head up and down, then shook his head from side to side but the pain not only stayed, it grew worse.

Hoot looked down. 'Odd,' he grunted, 'what's going on there?' Troubled, he swooped to Benny. 'Are you alright?' he asked, trying not to sound anxious.

'I... I think so,' Benny stammered, squinting with pain, 'but I have a sore head, Hoot, and it doesn't seem to be going away.'

'Confound this place,' Hoot grumbled. He had never heard of a unicorn with a headache. It didn't seem natural to him. He decided that the cause had to be something to do with Wish. Flying high, he scoured the ground with his owl's eyes of night. Nothing moved. All seemed fine.

Bobs soon noticed Benny's headshakes and it made him pause. He had seen this in a unicorn before but he couldn't think when or where.

What was the thing, Bobs mused, *that he should remember now?*

Bibs saw the pain in Benny's eyes. This was odd. The last he'd heard, unicorns didn't get sick or feel pain. Something strange was going on. Like a true guardian he stuck close to his charge and kept his eye on the low, dark places of the path.

Wish shone in all its glory. Trees lazed in the sun, sending blankets of shade over large striking boulders that were strewn charmingly across the road. The air was mellow and if it wasn't for Benny's problem, this walk through Wish looked easy enough. Then they turned a bend.

'You can't pass!' snarled a low, rasping growl.

Benny stopped. The pain in his forehead slammed in thumps. He looked at the ground and trees, but there was no one there.

'Who are you, where are you and why can't we pass?' Benny called out with the sureness that comes from being a unicorn.

'Not we, not we,' spat the voice. 'The owl and snails can do as they please, but no unicorn comes here!'

'No unicorn, but why?' Benny gasped, taken aback.

The voice narrowed to a hiss. 'You are hated, yes hated. You are hated and despised.'

The snails and Hoot drew sharp breaths. Unicorns, hated? Unicorns despised? What manner of creature was this?

Hoot began to speak, but Benny shushed him with a look. This was something new for Benny, indeed the very first time in all his life that he had ever met with hate. Swiftly he gathered his wits.

'But, you don't know me,' was his guarded response.

'I know you. You're a unicorn. Urgh!' croaked the voice.

Wise old Hoot had seen much in his day. Noting Benny's sad surprise, he took the matter in his hands.

'Why don't you show yourself, friend of owls and snails?' Hoot crooned. He had met many creatures, but never a hater of unicorns. It didn't seem possible that there could be such a thing.

The response was hoarse and chilling. 'Did I say I was a friend of owls and snails? I didn't say I was your friend. I just don't hate and despise you, that's all!'

'Ahh', Hoot sighed with his usual calm, 'not a friend? But you'd let us pass? I can't believe you'd care about such a little unicorn. Surely it's not like he could harm you in any way.'

Silence greeted the bewildered travellers.

Hoot tried again. 'Won't you at least come out from where you are so that I can thank you personally for granting the snails and myself permission to pass?'

But the owner of the voice spat and growled. 'Little unicorn? There's no such thing! Small or big they're all the same. Unicorns don't dare to come here ever, unless they wish to tempt their fate!' The last word was drawled as if the speaker had clenched teeth. 'Now, night bird,' it snarled thickly, 'if you're smart, you and those two sliding houses move on. Go, get out of here and be thankful that you can.'

'Sliding house indeed!' grumbled Bobs, as he wracked his brain. 'I know there's something I must remember. Think! Think!' he told himself. 'The problem is that I've had such a long, long life, with all sorts of memories in my head. Oh, it's on the edges of my mind but I need more time to work it out.'

'Sliding house?' mumbled Bibs. 'He must mean me and Bobs. If he wasn't so creepy-sounding and weird, I'd think that was kind of clever.' But Bibs didn't like this. No one could hate a unicorn. What would be the reason?

Benny was not going to make a fuss. His head pounded so badly that all he wanted was to escape. 'There must be several other roads I can take, so you all go ahead and I'll join you on the path another way,' he whispered to the others.

Hoot raised shocked eyes at Benny. 'I don't think so, Benny,' he declared. 'We should all turn around right now to look for another road.'

Benny reassured Hoot and the snails. 'Don't make a commotion. Let's pretend we aren't upset. Go on, and I'll meet you ahead. I'll just turn around and find another road. There's no need for the rest of you to go too far out of your way. After all, the wind tells us that this is the correct road to the Valley of Possibility.'

Bobs frowned. 'We can't leave you, young Benny. We're supposed to stay with you. That's what Coraggio said, you know.'

'I agree,' nodded Hoot. 'I'm not prepared to let you go galloping around on your own. This isn't the forest, Benny. This is Wish, after all.' Hoot peered over his shoulder as he said it. Then he crossed his wings and firmly stood his ground. *Benny was his charge!*

'It will only be for a moment,' Benny urged. 'There's no need to hold up the rest of you. I'll gallop back once you're through and find a way to catch up to you. You know I can. You know I'm fast.'

'We should all turn around,' Bibs joined in. 'Bobs is right, even though I gag to admit it.' He cringed, avoiding Bobs' eyes. 'If we lose you, Benny, Coraggio will punish us terribly, but not just that, we'd never forgive ourselves if you came to harm. There must be dozens of ways to reach the valley.'

Benny shook his head. 'You know I won't be far behind,' he urged. 'Have you ever known me to be slow? Have you ever known me to get lost?'

No one would argue about those things, but it was their job to stay by his side. Hoot didn't want to leave Benny, not even for a moment, but time was passing and decisions were thin on the ground, so he made a plan. He decided that he would only pretend to fly off, but in a crafty way, so that the owner of the growling voice would think he was going. Of course, he wouldn't really leave.

In a loud casual voice and with a large, obvious wink at Benny and the snails, Hoot announced, 'Come on then, forget Benny, we'll keep going.'

So, both snails, seeing Hoot was up to something, joined in the make-believe. Sighing casually and pretending not to worry, they played Hoot's game. Also winking at Benny, they crawled slowly past.

They all knew this was a bluff. They would never, ever just go away, not for any reason, and leave one of them behind. When they had agreed to come to Wish, they had known it could be a dangerous place but this journey was about seeking Hope and for that they needed to stick together, no matter what!

'So long, goodbye,' called Bibs and Bobs, as Hoot pretended to fly away.

'I'll catch up in just a tick,' Benny muttered. 'This should be easy enough.'

Benny turned his head, expecting his body to follow, but his hooves were stuck and he couldn't move. 'What mischief is this?' he grunted. Again, Benny tried to free his hooves, but the ground held tight and he couldn't budge!

Immediately, Hoot knew something was wrong. He swept low trying to see what was in the forest below.

In a greasy, gloating way, the hidden voice gurgled then called out loud.

'Ha-ha, you unicorns think you're so safe and so secure, but even your friends don't really care. Look, they had a choice, but they're leaving you all alone!'

It was the laughter that followed that stopped the

others in their tracks. It placed their hearts in shadow and gripped their minds with a terrible chill.

Hoot plunged, with piercing eyes, but he still couldn't see the enemy.

'Forgive me Coraggio,' Hoot breathed, 'I think we're in terrible trouble!' Distraught, he watched Benny buckle at the knees. *No time to lose*, he decided, *it's time to call for help!* Zooming as high as he dared, Hoot called out in a secret language known to flying friends; it was the call of the needy in the wild.

Bibs and Bobs stopped in their tracks. They peered around with dread. What manner of evil would do this to a unicorn?

'I knew we shouldn't have left him alone,' muttered Bobs. 'I knew we should *all* have gone another way. It's our fault, our fault for failing in our duty, and now Candela and Coraggio will have our heads!'

Bibs rolled his eyes. 'This isn't about fault,' he snapped. 'Things go wrong despite the best of plans. Anyway, if you'd stop feeling sorry for yourself, we could work out a way to help.'

Bobs frowned. 'What do you suggest we do, you youngster,' he spat.

'Well I guess we could put our thoughts together,' replied Bibs quietly, 'so if we stop fighting, that might be the best place for us to start, don't you think?'

The grunting voice scornfully roared at Benny. 'It serves you right! You unicorns think you're so superior! You think everyone loves you and believes you're great! Ha! You haven't got a chance!'

Benny was trapped and he knew it. The others would wait close by, but for now the fight was his. He wasn't afraid, because his heart was clear, and that came from being a unicorn. His delicate horn ached, though, almost blinding him with pain, so he racked his mind for what to do, and then recalled something he'd once heard.

Common unicorn lore stated that unicorn horns could purify water, and that was easy to remember as Benny did it most days just for fun, but there was other lore he had been taught, things he never thought he'd need.

'If evil grows out of control,' Candela had told him when he was a foal, 'unicorn horns ache in pain. That pain is our protection as it warns us to stay away.'

Benny remembered a bit more.

'Of course,' Candela had continued, 'some wicked, smelly things can't bear to know that true goodness lives, and in their minds they think happiness and truth must end. So if you should ever need to stay and fight, don't forget that also stored in your horn is all the power of the herd. It is the Ritual of Return.'

Protected from everyone's sight, the grunting noises of the enemy were interrupted with piercing laughter that pealed out and bounced from rocks, breaking them in two, then with plenty of wicked power left it split saplings where they grew.

Benny struggled to be free. His breath was harsh with panting gasps and his head hung low. The pain was crushing and his life force swayed but Benny braced his heart, mind and body for war.

Now unicorns by law don't fight, because they

honour peace and gentle kindness with all their might, but unicorn law also states that fear and evil can't go on. Benny knew that his enemy hated him, so he had to make a plan. He began to summon the Ritual of Return.

In a flash, Bobs suddenly knew what he needed to remember. 'I'm a fool,' he raged. 'A stupid old fool,' he cursed. 'We could have avoided this!' A lump rose in his throat. 'I've let them down! I've let the unicorns down! I asked to come so I could be of use, and Candela and Coraggio trusted me, especially since I'd been here before.' A picture of the unicorns flashed through his mind as they stood patiently with large, kind eyes.

'Forgive me, forgive me,' Bobs almost wept, 'let's hope we can escape.' He looked around to let Hoot know, but Hoot was so high in the sky that Bobs could barely see him. Annoyed, he knew he had to tell someone, so he called out to Bibs, but Bibs was nowhere to be seen. 'Blast!' he seethed. 'Where is everyone when you need them? Looks like I'll have to do everything myself, as usual.'

Bibs had made sure that no one was watching and then he'd snuck away. With stealth born to creatures such as him, he slid quickly yet silently, and reached a spot close to Benny. With one glance, he saw the little unicorn valiantly doing his best, even though Benny's legs wobbled and his breath came in shuddering gasps.

Good, Bibs thought, *Benny hasn't given up!*

It was true. Benny was focused on Candela and Coraggio and the unicorn herd. In his mind's eye he pictured them perfectly and with the vision came their power. It sent a small flare of strength through his bones, so his breathing eased and his knees grew stronger.

Bibs knew time was passing. He'd never met evil, but tactics were tactics, he decided. Moving slower than the slowest snail, he blended his shell to the landscape and pretended to be a rock. He carried his head low, so that no one could see his antenna or head, and grovelling, he made his way to the boulders in the clearing.

Chillingly, the enemy stopped garbling and began to chant. The droned words frightened the snails but Benny focused harder on the Ritual of Return.

Smoke flushed from the ground in slimy green clouds, as trees exploded then fell down dead. The sky began to brood as lightning cracked around Benny, but there was no sign of either thunder or rain. In just moments, the road that had been so peaceful was in a state of noise and ruin.

Reaching the spot he wanted, Bibs stood quaking in his shell. He'd just seen what they were fighting. He'd just seen their enemy!

CHAPTER 7

There is no time; there is no time

A tremendous wave of water gushed upward from the pond as an enraged Oobaat surfaced, sending water flying everywhere.

'What have you done, Rana the frog?' Oobaat bellowed. 'What did you do, you dingbat of an amphibian?' He plunged over to where Rana sat, and pushed his tortoise beak into the horrified frog's face. 'Because of your selfish desire to show off, that girl and her dog may be lost forever!'

'No, no, no,' whimpered a cringing Rana. 'I wrote their names on the lily leaves. You know, just the way I've seen you do.'

'Did you tell them how dangerous it is?' Oobaat hollered, as Rana squirmed.

'A bit,' Rana winced, wishing he were dead.

'A bit! You either did or you didn't, foolish frog! There's no *a bit*, about going to Wish!' Oobaat shuddered.

Wish came from the minds of humans. Any visitor who went unprepared might vanish with those thoughts. The whole thing didn't bear thinking about! Quickly, before time ran out, Oobaat checked that Rana had indeed recorded Rielle and Pud's names, and also their time of passing through. The right way of doing things was their only hope, and it might make all the difference yet.

'Which leaf, frog?' Oobaat snapped.

Rana crawled to show him the one. No bounce or jump or showing off now.

Oobaat breathed a mighty sigh of relief. *The names were recorded.* They were roughly written, but Rielle and Pud were there. The girl and her dog wouldn't disappear after all!

Something similar had happened once, nearly a thousand years before. It had to be fixed then, and it would have to be fixed now. Honourable Oobaat knew what he must do. The wishing pond would have to be shut for now and a ban would be put on it until he returned from fixing this mess. He turned to the downcast Rana. With brows furrowed, and in a steely voice, Oobaat glared at the unfortunate frog.

'I *must* follow them into Wish. I must make sure they know the rules, and most importantly, I must be sure that the girl doesn't do anything foolish, rash or... human.'

Rana nodded and shed a small dramatic tear.

Infuriated, Oobaat quietly rasped, 'Your punishment while I'm gone will be to guard this wishing pond.' His piercing stare bored into Rana. He paused, willing his words to make their mark. 'If you let anyone in, and I mean *anyone*, I promise I will see to it that you disappear in a puff of smoke!' Oobaat paused again. Then, with a grimace, he continued. 'Meaning, in case you don't get my drift, that what was once Rana the frog will become tiny, trivial airborne particles!'

Rana wasn't sure whether to be pleased or not. After all, he was getting a second chance, right? Then his heart closed over and he began to quake. *Airborne particles?* This was the worst punishment in the world! What if he couldn't resist? What if he let someone else in, just like before?

'Please, I'd rather not,' Rana whispered. 'I'd rather not have to mind the pond. Punish me any other way you like, but I'd rather not have to face the temptation.'

Rielle and Pud's danger made Oobaat ruthless. 'While you sit here all safe and snug,' the gatekeeper warned, ignoring Rana, 'keep in mind the possible doom to the girl and the dog.' He took a deep breath. 'If they are harmed from your lack of warning, it will not only be on your head, but also on mine.' His eyes flailed the frog. 'So get it right this time, Rana, or you will become nothing but dust, and it will be your own doing!'

'But,' Rana sheepishly pleaded, 'can you give me some tips, then, before you go? You know, so I won't do the wrong thing and go up in,' he quivered, 'er, smoke?' He put on his most appealing expression and sent a huge tear to flow down his face.

'Ah,' smiled Oobaat, without joy, 'I have every faith in you, Rana.' He sighed. 'Because I know that self-preservation will be the first thing on your mind. Don't worry,' he finished with another grim look, 'I'm sure you'll manage to work it out.' Then, without another word, Oobaat dove back into the pond and swam away to find Rielle and Pud.

Oobaat really cared about the silly show-off of a frog, but broken trust had to be redeemed. A grin spread on Oobaat's ancient face. He hoped that one day even Rana might become a sensible chap. It might not happen soon, but maybe one day.

What Rana didn't know was that the gatekeeper had placed a ban on the pond, and there wasn't a soul in any world that would even know the pond was there. Rana would be thinking, and that was punishment enough! All alone back at the pond, Rana perched on a lily pad. His goggle eyes darted back and forth as more tears of self-pity washed down his face. He croaked, but no one answered. Resigned, he sat down for the long, hard wait.

...

'Oh, Pud,' Rielle breathed blissfully as she took in the beauty of Wish's sandy shore. 'It's exactly as I imagined it would be!'

Pud was wet and cold. Where they'd come from it was the middle of the night, and here they were in the brightness of day. He just wanted to sleep in a warm, dark place. Exasperated, he glanced at Rielle.

Of course it's exactly as you thought, he mused grumpily. *This is Wish; you are a human and I suppose it's what you want it to be.* Then, determined to drain the water from his ears, Pud attempted to stand on his head.

Rielle grimaced. 'Urgh,' she winced, as if she'd only just noticed, 'I'm all wet and grubby.' She grabbed a handful of her hair and scowled as she tried to comb it with her fingers. 'Between that stormy night and this,' she sighed,

'I don't think I've ever been so dirty in my life!'

'Tell me about it,' grunted Pud.

'What are you doing?' Rielle frowned as she watched Pud stick his bottom in the air. She decided that her dog was becoming very unusual. It looked for the entire world like he was trying to stand on his head, but dogs didn't do that kind of thing.

Suddenly, Pud jumped up with a huge grin on his face. He wagged his tail wildly then he leapt and bound like a puppy just before it finds disgrace. His weird contortions had worked; the water had drained from his ears! He shook his coat as hard as he could, spraying water all over Rielle. Then with a broad grin, Pud ran dodging, away.

Rielle gasped at the new onslaught of cold water just as she thought she was starting to dry. 'Argh!' she squealed. Then, with joyful abandon, she and Pud played tag and chase on the shores of Wish.

Stepping from a line of trees, the baby faun played his flute. As he tiptoed along the shore, his music beckoned them to follow. Golden rods of musical notes shot from his mellow pipes disguised as fingers of afternoon sun. Unaware, Pud and Rielle chased each other in lively high spirits. The sun shone hot and the shore lapped gently and before they knew it, they were dry. As suddenly as he'd appeared, the gentle faun stepped away from the shores. Rielle and Pud sat down breathless, to rest. Rielle looked around. They were a long way from where they'd landed.

'I'm hungry,' Rielle told Pud, 'and I'm sure you are

too, but we really are supposed to be looking for the others, so I suppose we'll find food soon enough.' She weighed up their surroundings. 'It's so lovely here, Pud,' she sighed.

Pud wrinkled his nose and frowned. Rielle didn't notice.

'Wouldn't it be perfect if we never had to leave?' Rielle whispered with a glistening eye.

Pud wasn't having any of that! Candela in her wisdom had guessed the future of Rielle's thoughts and had passed them with mind-power on to Pud. Knowing what those thoughts could be, Pud had hoped they wouldn't surface. He just wanted to find the others, find Hope and get the blazes out of there! Why was his mistress being difficult again? With a dog-wish of his own, he hoped that the others were close by and that they might find them very soon.

In the distance, as if in answer to Pud's wish, the piping faun picked up his pipes. So softly that even Pud's ears barely heard it, the music burst into swing. Set free, the music hunted for Rielle and her dog. Some notes scoured the ground like trackers on a scent. Others flew above the trees and, like hawks, tried to sight the pair.

Pud tilted his head, looking up, first to one side and then the other.

'What are you looking at?' Rielle asked, as once again, the notes disguised themselves and shot the air like bolts of sunlight.

Pud followed the melody.

'Wait for me!' Rielle called. Something familiar caught her attention. 'Pud, Pud,' she exclaimed, 'can you smell that scent of almond blossoms?'

So it was, in this unwitting way, that they left the sand dunes and the shore, to follow the little faun's deliberate trail.

...

Oobaat plunged onto the shores of Wish. He looked around but couldn't see the girl or her dog. He lumbered and laboured on the hot, thick sand and his large, wise eyes scowled with concern.

'I'm fast in the water but so slow on land. I'll never find them at this rate, and the girl must be told the rules *soon*, or she stands to make all manner of trouble for herself, not to mention anyone else.'

Again he scoured the beach, but Rielle and Pud were nowhere in sight. Oobaat pondered briefly and then with a weighty sigh, he made a decision.

He began to chant:

Spirit, fire, air, earth and water
Moon, stars, sun and sky

Give me might
Make it right

Swift of speed
Like birds in flight

Not for nothing
Do I ask

Time is needed
For my task

Send me forth
Brisk and swift

Until my mission is complete
This I humbly do entreat.

Oobaat waited. His thoughts and memory were still the same; however, he knew he was different when the sun felt hot on his body, even though he didn't feel as if he'd actually changed. He decided that the best test was to move. Judging distance on how he usually walked as a tortoise, he willed his body to reach a grove of trees. Before he'd almost finished with the thought, he was already there.

'Success,' he grinned, 'and, taking a guess, I'm the same as I was the last time I needed to change my shape.' Quickly now, for there was no time to lose, he looked around, sniffed the ground, then smelled the air. He looked to the right.

'Ah, almond blossom,' he smiled, 'time to go, Oobaat, old mate.' His graceful new body followed the thought. Oobaat the noble gatekeeper now travelled with speed, doing his best to track Rielle and Pud.

...

Rielle puffed as she chased after her leggy dog. 'The Valley of Possibility, Pud!' she called to remind him, but

Pud was already following the scent.

The little faun looked back, and seeing that Pud was on the right track, he cast the girl and the dog a parting look. Gathering his notes back to his pipes, he vanished into Wish.

Fixed on following the smell of almond blossoms, Pud willed Rielle to hurry. He wanted to find Benny so that Hope could be found. The sooner this journey was over, the less chance there would be for his mistress to find trouble. He looked back from time to time to check that she was fine, then lead the way as fast as he could.

'Pud,' Rielle called suddenly, 'over there in the distance. It looks like a storm.'

They paused to look. Pud sniffed the air. For some minutes they stood together silently, not daring to guess what they were seeing. The distant sky was red. Even from where they were, they could see clouds that boiled and bunched as lightning bolts crashed to earth. Pud sniffed again. Strange, he could usually smell a storm, but all he could smell was fire. Goose bumps raised themselves on Rielle's arms. Pictures of Benny flashed through her mind. Jittery with unease, she shivered.

'Come on, Pud,' Rielle whispered, 'it's got nothing to do with us, so let's keep going.' Thoughts of Benny didn't leave her mind though.

Pud trembled in his heart. He hoped their friends were safe. Hastily, they turned away and began to run again.

'Whatever it is,' Rielle breathed, 'we don't want to be caught in its fury.' But dread sat for a long time on both of them. They continued to run.

They now followed a level, beaten track. Puzzled, Rielle wondered why she was finding it hard to breathe. It was as if the very air wasn't nourishing enough. Pud seemed unaffected, but Rielle was struggling.

Then the track pitched into a natural avenue. As if a switch had been pulled, Rielle and Pud plunged from sunlight into one of nature's darkened halls. Before them, a line of lofty trees clasped a long, winding road. Rielle strained her eyes to see the end of it, but the avenue kept fast, countless trees.

Standing tall, like proprietors in a contract of binding ownership, the trees oozed stability and power. Brimming with hidden poetry that ebbed and flowed from the ages, they paid their dues to a tantalizing, mysterious truth that spoke of endless days and long, inspired nights, as they tenderly reached up to a welcoming sky.

If Rielle had held hands with six friends just like her, it would have barely been possible to circle each tree. This tribute to their endurance and respectful bearing made Rielle feel small and somewhat daunted. Never again would she take trees for granted, not since Old Poky had saved them from the abyss. Although these were different in shape and size, they bore a resemblance to that old tree, the resemblance of shelter and paternal strength.

Pud peered up and slowed from his jogging. In a show of reverence to majesty seen and sensed, he walked quietly on.

Rielle wanted to run as fast as she could to escape this awe-inspiring place. Her feet and legs stopped for themselves though, as exhausted, she looked up.

Uncannily, she wondered if the trees read the secrets of her heart. The trees remained aloof with their feet firmly planted in the ground.

'Why is it,' Rielle whispered to Pud, 'that I'm always the noisy one in these quiet places?'

Pud's tongue lolled in lazy restfulness, dropping saliva to the ground. His mistress was right. It did seem that she was always the noisy one. He grinned at her and placed his paw onto her shoe.

'I was scared here at first,' Rielle muttered, as they moved on, 'but I don't think this is an unfriendly place, Pud.' She listened, but no birds chirped and the breeze, if there was one, must have been singing so far above them that there could be no promise of it ever being heard. Blossom scent still beckoned with mischievous wafts. 'At least I think it's not unfriendly,' she murmured with a shiver, 'although it seems unnaturally still, don't you think?' Pud didn't really care; he just wanted to keep moving. 'Come on then,' Rielle stated, doing her best to remain cheery. So saying, she placed a protective hand on Pud's noble head as they made their reverent way through the humbling vastness of the avenue's cathedral.

At last, as if through the eternity of ages, where stories of once-upon-a-time joined with now, they reached the end of the avenue. Surprised, Rielle found that she was reluctant to leave. Stopping and looking back, she marvelled at the dignity and stamina of the place.

'Goodbye,' she whispered sadly. Profound silence was her answer.

Sunlight bit their eyes as they stepped from the avenue back into the day.

'Arh!' Rielle gasped at the sudden onslaught, and Pud hid his face behind a paw. Blinking hard, Rielle was surprised to see it was just an ordinary day. She looked back at the avenue, amazed that despite it being made of trees, it presented to the world a solid wall.

'I didn't realise how easy it became to see in the dark,' she mused.

Pud opened his eyes, squinted, and then barked. Rielle hardly heard him as she looked pensively back at the avenue. Was something moving back there? She strained to see but couldn't be sure. Maybe it was just a trick of the light, perhaps a shifting and changing of the sun on the ground? She shivered. A strange feeling passed under her skin. For the first time since arriving in Wish, Rielle began remembering what the unicorns had said.

Wish is an ever-changing land because it exists from the minds of humans… from the minds of humans… from the minds of humans!

With a jolt of heartfelt longing, Rielle pictured the beautiful herd. They had been uneasy when Wish was mentioned, and the memory of their misgivings made small hairs stand on her neck.

'From the minds of humans? Well, that could mean anything, really,' she reflected in a whimsical voice. But a cloud covered her heart.

Pud stopped barking.

'Thoughts are funny things really, Pud,' Rielle murmured.

Pud began to bellow again.

As if waking from a trance, Rielle finally heard him. She tore her eyes from the avenue. 'What is it?' she asked, frowning at the dog.

Pud became silent.

Rielle looked around and then saw for herself. Below them, in a valley of serene damask, created by vast forests of blossoming trees, there nestled a fortress. The air brimmed with vibrant, tantalising sweetness, as if all the cake shops in the world had gathered together and baked special treats.

'The Valley of Possibility,' Rielle breathed. 'Oh, it must be, Pud! Just look at the trees. Those are almond trees, aren't they? There must be thousands of them.' She took a deep exaggerated breath. 'This place smells good enough to eat.' Her words trailed. Hesitation filled her heart.

'We're here so soon, and any minute now we'll see the others. Won't they be surprised that we've come here too?' She considered the building. 'It doesn't look so big,' she murmured. 'It's surrounded by a moat. I wonder how we get in. Oh... how cute, there's a little wooden bridge.' Rielle paused, and instead of moving on, as at first she thought she would, a kind of lethargy filled her bones. 'I just need to sit for a moment, Pud. I'm very tired, you know, and hungry again, of course.' She grinned awkwardly.

Pud sat and licked his paws. He needed a drink, but a rest would do.

Rielle squinted at the beauty below, her thoughts jumbling.

'Hope's in there, Pud.' Her eyes held clouds in them, and her voice stuck in her throat. 'How will I know him?

Or her?' she said, correcting herself in sudden shock. 'Benny didn't say who... or what... Hope is, or even what Hope looks like.' She finished the sentence with surprise. 'Of course, I really don't know what I'm looking for, do I? So I can't be blamed if I don't find Hope, can I?'

'It's best, Rielle,' Candela had gently prompted, 'if you leave this journey to Benny and his helpers, and that you take your faithful Pud and return to sleep. '

A twinge of guilt tugged at Rielle. Dearest, beautiful Candela!

'Go to bed, young Rielle,' Candela had encouraged. 'All will be well, you'll see.'

The small hairs on Rielle's neck stirred and a quiver inched along her spine. She looked at Pud, but his eyes were locked on something behind her. He whined loudly, looked up at his mistress, then turned and looked back again.

'What is it?' Rielle whispered, as doubts made their mark.

Pud remained silent with a gathered brow.

Rielle forced herself to stand up calmly. She heard an unfamiliar sound but she wasn't too worried. After all, how bad could it be? She had met unicorns and guard snails and frogs that could talk, so, calmly, she turned and looked behind her. Something green-ish was moving in the grass.

'Hello?' she asked, before she heard the sound again. Puzzled, she whispered as she glanced at Pud. 'Is that a dragging sound, do you think, Pud?'

Pud whined but didn't look scared. Rielle took a step.

'Look out,' a voice called gruffly, 'you're almost stepping on my face.'

'Who are you?' Rielle asked, stopping in her tracks. The grass was too long for her to see well, so she waited.

Sure enough, the voice called out cheerily. 'We haven't met, but just a tick, wait on please and I'll join you soon.'

Mystified, Rielle waited as loud rustling and grunts came from the grass.

'Almost there,' the voice called. Then rearing from the grass, there shot up a head. 'Hello,' it cried. 'You're just the person I've been looking for!'

Rielle gaped. In one critical moment, terror gripped her heart. Levelling its great yellow eyes at the same height as her own, and wiggling an enormous thick neck, a huge snake poked the air with its tongue.

Pud barked and jumped up and down, but Rielle didn't stop to think. She took a step back, turned and ran.

'Wait, wait!' called the snake.

Fear lent wings to Rielle, and screaming, she cried, 'Run, Pud, run, ruuuuun!' Bolting down the sleepy, sun-drenched slope of the hill, she headed straight for the Tower of Dreams. It was not for Pud to question why, and with a quick last look at the snake, he galloped after her.

Behind them on the hill, Oobaat sighed. 'Oh dear, I forgot that part,' he groaned. 'I forgot that humans aren't too friendly. I especially forgot that they're odd about snakes. Ah well, I can't be worried about changing into something else. I'll just have to find another way to make the girl listen so that I can do my job.'

Rielle thundered noisily across the little wooden

bridge, and hurtled over the moat. Her eyes darted every which way, as she stormed through the door of the Tower of Dreams.

'Benny!' she called, as she tore through the halls. 'Benny! Benny! Is anyone here? Has anyone seen a unicorn?'

CHAPTER 8

Redemption

A rainbow dragon on the wing heard Hoot's desperate cries of need. Swooping with lively, reckless abandon, he joined the owl in the giant wasteland of Wish's sky.

'I heard *The Call*,' he cried, his piercing yellow eyes sparkling. 'I am Flightlord, from my mother Flightprincess, and my father, Skylord.'

Anticipating the thrill of a challenge, the dragon flapped his streamlined wings. Then he bowed politely to Hoot, as they rode the currents of the wind. Although only a baby rainbow dragon, proven by the tuft of curly hair growing on his chin, he was fabulously handsome, with pale green scales that looked like mother of pearl.

Flightlord's nostrils flared as he flexed his long talons and magnificent claws. His body rippled with muscle and power, and his wings spanned many metres, but he was still a baby after all, at only about a hundred and three. He peered good-naturedly at Hoot, knowing that he could eat the owl with just one bite, but he had no such intention. Owls were known to be wise and learned, and served a better purpose than dragon suppers.

Hoot understood that this was only a baby dragon, as elder male rainbow dragons had long grey beards and the ladies had short black manes, but he didn't underestimate the majestic creature. Desperate for help, yet with a somewhat nervous bow, he replied.

'Hoot GreyOwl at your service.'

Flying together, they found the highest bough of the strongest tree to discuss what was happening below. Not for them a flimsy sapling. They couldn't risk being blown to bits. Forgetting his fears, Hoot quickly told Flightlord why he needed his help.

Flightlord pinned Hoot with sharp, bright eyes, listening with a keen wit and mind. Swiftly, he grasped what was going on. In the private language known to flying friends and with a voice poised in secret mystery and furtive menace, he proceeded to tell what it was he knew.

'It's like this,' he began. 'For aeons *he* has guarded the path on which the unicorn now stands. We all avoid him, each one of us, because he's stranger than we know.'

Hoot frowned anxiously. 'What creature is he?'

Flightlord nodded. 'Many years ago,' he explained, 'a human warrior made a wish. He said he was the son of a king... a prince, I think they call them. He was a greedy boy. He was very blessed for a human but he wanted more.' Flightlord's eyes glittered shrewdly. 'He had excellent health, perfect looks, great stores of human gold, and apparently his people loved him, but it seems that wasn't enough.'

Gripped in the tale, Hoot listened, but his eyes never left Benny below.

'The prince,' continued Flightlord, 'wished so hard and longed so much, that he was answered... he burst onto the shores of Wish. Apparently, he had one desire. He wanted the horn of a unicorn. He believed that a unicorn horn could give magic to anyone who claimed it.'

Hoot stared in horror. He had heard that hunters chased and slayed unicorns for their horns long ago, but he hadn't been sure that such barbaric tales of cruelty and waste were really true.

'Well that's ridiculous!' Hoot exclaimed. 'Everyone knows that unicorn horns give power only to the unicorns.'

Peals of wild laughter reached their ears and Wish grew dark as the sky thundered and boiled amongst corrupt clouds.

The dragon nodded in tight-lipped response. 'I'll make the story short,' he promised. 'There was a sorcerer who lived in Wish at the same time that the warrior prince charged its shores. Everyone called this sorcerer the *Sorcerer of Content*, for he had spent many ages practising harmless magic, showing nothing but friendship. However, beneath his gracious facade, there seemed to have stirred deeper longings. It appears that his hidden heart felt a sense of great self importance. No one will ever know what he was thinking, because with a strange and bizarre twist that sometimes happens, he let the prince bribe him with treasure.' Flightlord paused, making sure Hoot followed the story. 'The sorcerer's task,' he went on, 'was to lure a unicorn to the prince, so that the prince could kill it and steal its prized horn.'

Hoot sucked his breath in a gasp of shock.

Flightlord shrugged. 'And yet,' he continued, in a puzzled voice, 'the sorcerer forgot the most important thing, which he really should have known. He forgot the truth of unicorns.'

The dragon peered at Hoot with a faraway look. Then, with his yellow eyes flashing, he went on. 'So it was that a unicorn walked into their trap, but just as it seemed they would succeed, she tricked them both, catching them out in their plan. Cleverly she left them then, to their misery, and fled back to the unicorn herd.'

Hoot cut in. 'Is there hope for young Benny?'

Flightlord answered urgently. 'That creature below, whom we now call the *Sorcerer of Great Contempt*, has been like this ever since. His rage lives on, for he has never forgiven being caught out and tricked by a unicorn.' The dragon's voice caught in his throat as foreboding coloured the air. 'He has waited a very long time to make good his revenge, so there's no more time to lose, Hoot the owl. He will do his best to destroy your friend, the little unicorn.'

Fervently, Hoot asked, 'What happened to the prince?'

Flightlord hung his head. 'No longer a prince or a problem to us,' he murmured in a hushed tone.

In the meantime, in the forest below, Bobs searched high and low for what he knew he had to find. 'Why, oh why,' he groaned, 'didn't Candela warn Benny about this evil?'

Deep down, though, Bobs knew that unicorns did everything with a purpose. Clearly this was Benny's journey and each experience was his to learn. Candela had done the next best thing, and that was to send companions along to help steer him on his course. That's why Coraggio had checked whether the snails understood the importance of their job.

'I should have remembered about this,' Bobs muttered as he kept searching. 'It's really my fault. I'm a terrible companion, a failure, and a fool!'

On the path, Benny focused on the herd, remembering all the good things that they were. To the naked eye, nothing had changed. Benny still swayed unsteadily on his feet, a little unicorn alone and bent. However, for anyone with special sight, Benny was now surrounded in white misty light: the Ritual of Return!

Bibs had ground to a halt. The heat and stifling air were the least of his problems even though they made it difficult to move. His hunch had been right. He had found the enemy! He was excited that his daring had paid off, but horrified by what he saw.

Cleverly hiding in an overhang of a large boulder and tucked into a small nook, there burrowed the strangest creature. It was a beast so ugly that Bibs could hardly bear to look. It had a slobbering head, half dog, half something else and the body of a human.

But then Bibs heard it growl and speak, all the words jumbling in its throat. 'No, no,' it croaked, 'that won't do. If I'm a wolf I won't have hands!' Stunned, Bibs watched the creature change back into itself.

Shrivelled and bent, with shadowed livid eyes and limp, raggedy hair, sat a strange, human-like thing. It babbled odd words and chants, all the while waving its gnarled hands around. When its temper rose, it cast spells that turned the sky to fire, burnt innocent trees and broke ancient stones. Gurgling and belching, it was hard to understand what it said, but after what seemed like particularly pleasing thoughts, with flashing eyes and grunting noises, it laughed loudly with glee.

Bibs cringed and shrunk. *He had to warn the others!*

The air and the ground were becoming so hot that Bibs' naturally moist tummy was drying up. He needed his slimy trail, otherwise he couldn't slide. With the greatest effort, Bibs tried to leave, but instead, he jerked, jigged and bunny-hopped. He shuddered. *The creature was bound to see him if he couldn't get out of there, and then he would cook Bibs, just like he was doing to the trees and rocks!*

Young Bibs didn't know he was being brave when he had decided to investigate. All he thought of in this troubled time was that Benny the unicorn needed his friends.

Candela in her wisdom had chosen well, after all.

At last, Bobs found what he wanted! For one relieved, heartfelt moment, he caught his breath and examined his sought-after prize. There, all alone by the side of the road where no other trees would grow, was a bushy shrub with dark green leaves prettily flecked with edges of gold. They were the leaves Bobs needed, but the bush was taller and much higher than he remembered.

'Typical,' he frowned, 'typical, typical, typical! Just because I want them, the blinky leaves are out of reach.'

He sighed. 'This is my punishment. It's got to be my punishment for having a memory like a sieve.'

Bobs peered around. Then, sure he was alone and that no one was watching, he bared his teeth and jumped as high as he could. Comically, which his proud heart hated, he discovered that if he did a kind of bounce and jump, he could just reach the leaves and quickly bite them off. After several leaps and painful landings, with the leaves in his teeth, he fled to find Benny.

'If anyone saw me,' he squirmed grumbling, 'I'll deny that was me bouncing about, no matter what!' His underbelly was bruised from all the silly jumping, but worst of all, so was his pride.

Close by Benny, Bibs shuddered, amazed at what he was hearing.

'Last time,' the creature babbled, 'the unicorn escaped, but not this time, not this time, no, because this time,' it pealed into wilful laughter, 'I'm going to lasso it.' It screeched with joy. 'Yes, brilliant, brilliant, I have brilliant ideas! I'll lasso it around that clean white neck and then the unicorn will be my slave!' It drooled and gurgled.

Bibs went cold.

'Then,' Bibs heard him chortle, 'when I am ready, we will find a way to kill it, and then we shall see!'

Bibs watched in wide-eyed dismay as the creature uprooted a patch of grass, just because it could.

Bibs choked down fear. Benny a slave? Benny dead? *It's now or never*, he decided. *There's no more time to lose! We aren't having our unicorn caught. Not if I can help it, that's for sure.*

Shadows stretched across Benny's path. Ash and burnt timber tumbled overhead to land on the ground around him. Bits of ash fell on his curly mane, singeing his coat and tail. He thought of the Ritual of Return as if that was all that mattered. Then, slowly, so slowly, Benny moved one hoof, and another and another. He was free! He breathed deeply and stood up straight. He stretched his neck, raised his face and straightened his knees. He was ready to fight or flee! The creature wasn't watching Benny. Boldly humming to itself with strange gestures, it busily made a long length of rope. Pleased with the result, it grunted and gushed. Then, in front of Bibs' astonished eyes, the creature waved its hands, chanted a verse and turned itself into an impressive warrior wearing fabulous armour.

Bibs trembled so hard that he could barely move.

Standing tall, the creature looked piercingly at the angry sky. Holding the rope carefully as if it were his treasure, he whispered words to it. The rope twitched and then it pulsed. Slowly, deliberately, it began to curl, snake-like, through the air.

Bibs choked. 'He's no creature,' he breathed. 'He's a sorcerer, a wicked wizard or something like that.' Bibs felt his heart thump and bump. 'Does he know I'm here?'

The sorcerer chuckled. 'This should be easy,' he murmured, gloating. 'With its teensy, weensy hooves stuck to the path, I'll quickly lasso that clean white neck.' Only then did he turn to Benny.

Through the forest Bobs raced, even though he'd become lost twice, bumped his nose, fallen down holes and climbed out again. With the leaves still clutched in his teeth, he reached the spot where Benny stood.

At that very moment Bibs bolted past, horror sketched on his face.

Just then Hoot, too, swooped with Flightlord from their treetop place.

With speed and purpose, the friends united, and it was only just in time.

Roaring at the top of his voice, Bibs, the silly, young, brave snail, called and called again. 'Be careful, Benny, he's got a thick lasso to catch you with! Run! Run if you can!'

Bobs grunted. *Had the foolish youngster forgotten that Benny's feet were stuck?*

The sorcerer gaped. Deeply buried in his spells and thoughts, he had assumed the snails and owl were long gone. At first he didn't understand, and then, amazed at their daring, it dawned on him that the unicorn's friends had hatched a plan.

'They dare to defy *me*,' he scorned. 'They dare to defy me. Fools! Don't they know anything? Don't they know the things I can do?' With fuming, livid eyes he bared his teeth in a demented grin. 'A snail,' he snarled, 'a snail is running amok!' Then with a snap of his neck he quickly looked to where Benny stood. Fury rippled through the sorcerer's skin. Somehow, the unicorn was standing tall!

Defiantly, Benny faced him, his legs straight, his strong neck arched.

'No time to lose!' roared the sorcerer. Pointing at

Benny, he shrieked:

By muddied shore
And darkest hour
I seek to defeat
I seek power
By withered nose and smelly feet
Up, up, embroiled rope
Go, cast your way
And bring me victory
On this day!

With a howl of wrath, he twirled the rope into the bitter brown sky.

But Benny was free. Heeding Bibs' timely warning, he bunched himself and leapt away.

The rope uncurled with a hissing noise and struck out like a snake to bite, almost grasping Benny's neck. It arched and soared with unusual grace, as marked by evil, it followed the scent of unicorn blood, hunting Benny wherever he leapt.

Benny jumped sideways and once more escaped, but with an almost lazy twist, the rope glided with ease, chasing poor Benny twice as hard! Benny ran with all his speed and everyone knew that was great indeed, but the rope grew and lengthened, and listened with care, as its master told it fierce words. Benny almost made it; he nearly ran away, but the sorcerer was a sorcerer after all and the magic rope kept twisting through the air.

'Run, Benny!' called the others.

Too late! The rope caught one of Benny's back legs, biting it hard and not letting go. For futile moments Benny fought, but in doing so, the rope cut deeper.

'I've got you now, unicorn!' bawled the sorcerer with delight, but again he'd taken too much for granted, for he'd forgotten all about Hoot, you see.

At last, Flightlord saw his chance. Diving fiercely to do his part, swooping down with Hoot in tow, soaring through the soot-stained air, the dragon sent a shaft of fire to slice and burn through the thick lasso.

Benny's leg was bleeding as the sorcerer urged his rope to hold, but the dragon was valiant and brave of heart and he put up the most wonderful show!

Alas, though, the rope was magic and it barely noticed the dragon fire.

Urging his rope to hold as he threw bolts of evil through the sky, the sorcerer cursed the dragon with words of damnation and power. The sky grew black. The ground boiled as trees burst into flame and stones turned into molten rock. Fury unleashed as the wind screamed and moaned with despair.

Flightlord wasn't giving up. This was what dragons called serious fun! So again and again he breathed fire on the rope, but all the while he made a silent plan. He was a dragon, after all, swift of wing and stubborn in heart, born to play with fire, and bred for war.

Relishing the challenge of a good, true battle, he dodged the sorcerer's spells and curses. He flew so hard, so fast and so sleekly that Hoot stopped following and watched from safety. The rainbow dragon breathed careful fire. He couldn't risk burning Benny. He breathed it wherever he could on the rope, but the rope kept jousting with clever skill.

And then, with a daring that made Benny, Hoot, Bibs and Bobs gasp, Flightlord tried something that amazed them all. He pretended that he'd been hit by a spell, and let himself fall in a coiled lump. The sorcerer roared in triumph, but he underestimated the baby rainbow dragon.

Just before Flightlord hit the ground, he uncoiled with tremendous strength, and furiously aiming at the sorcerer, he breathed a great ball of dragon fire. The fireball hit the sorcerer's arm and the rope went limp, then promptly dissolved!

A cheer went up from Benny's friends. Benny was free! But the rope had cut deeply into his leg and all he could do was painfully limp.

It was Bobs' turn to show his stuff. Although the molten ground scorched him, he slid with faithful speed to the little unicorn.

'Quick Benny, eat these leaves,' he called. 'They're magic and they'll heal your wound.'

Puzzled, Benny began to chew the leaves.

'Don't chew them,' bellowed a frustrated Bobs, 'we don't have time! Just swallow them and we'll be on our way.'

With no time to argue, Benny did as he was told. With a sigh of surprise the others watched, as his leg repaired perfectly with no visible scar!

'I'll explain some other time,' yelled Bobs. 'Now run, Benny, run!'

'Come on, I'll lead you,' called triumphant Flightlord. 'We must escape as fast as we can!'

The little band turned and fled.

Behind them a wail and a screech tore the air. The Sorcerer of Great Contempt grovelled on the ground. 'You haven't seen the last of me,' he shrieked. 'You haven't lost me yet! I'm coming after you, unicorn, and next time, I'll win!'

Sickly air swirled around them as wild fire burned out of control.

'Follow me!' called Flightlord, and at this time in their hour of need, they let him show the way.

Following as fast as they could through the blackened and burning land, they all shared the same thought. *Had they left the sorcerer behind or was he hot on their trail?* They had learned never to take anything for granted because no one could ever be too clever, or too sure.

Guiding the fleeing four, Flightlord didn't stop or slow the pace for what seemed to the others an unbearably long time. Eventually, though, he noticed that the others were struggling. Slowing in midair, Flightlord checked in all directions. His impeccable vision told him that no one was following, so he swooped to join the bedraggled crew.

Nestled in the hollow of a hill, scrubby trees that weren't much to look at did a perfect job of screening them. Flightlord was sad that it was over. So much fun in one day! 'I don't see anyone following us,' he whispered,' so it might be best if you stop to rest here for a while.'

Hoot perched on a low tree branch that let him see up, and let him see down, with a clear view side to side.

Bibs and Bobs collapsed and lay sprawled with their sore, burnt bellies in the air. Benny did his best to catch his breath.

Flightlord sighed and scratched himself, checking to see if all his scales were in place. *I need lunch after that little skirmish,* he decided. *There's nothing like battle for making an appetite.* He watched the others with yellow eyes, revelling with pride in a job well done.

'I'll have to leave you here, my friends,' he cautioned. 'I believe that for now, you'll be quite safe.'

Benny was barely recognisable with his body and face covered in soot, but he still had the dignity of a unicorn. He bowed low with respect.

'Esteemed dragon, I'll cherish what you've done and always be grateful. You chanced your life for us and put your own safety in doubt. For that, you'll always be known as a special friend to unicorns.'

Flightlord bowed back. 'It was an honour and the least that I could do, young Benny,' he replied. 'I owed your mother, Candela, a favour, and I am glad to repay her by having helped you.' The dragon flared his scaly nose.

'Flightlord,' panted Hoot, 'son of Skyprincess and mighty Skylord, I will forever be grateful that you answered my call. Without you, I'm not sure how things might have gone.'

Flightlord nodded. 'Goodbye everyone, stay safe and don't forget, Hoot knows the words if you should need my help again.' Then, with one swift push, he flew away to where it is that dragons live, work and play, by day.

Benny looked puzzled. 'My mother?' he asked. 'What

do you think he meant by that, Hoot?'

The owl shook himself. 'I'm not sure,' he replied with a quizzical look, 'but one day, I think you'll find out.'

Benny realised there was so much more to everything than he had ever imagined when he was in the forest. Sending one last look to the disappearing dragon, he turned back to his friends.

Poor Bibs and Bobs were blackened with soot all over, and sore from sliding over hot molten ground. Hoot, who was usually so neat and tidy had a black, soot-stained eye as if he'd been fighting fisticuffs.

Despite the hardship and the horror, the four travellers stared at each other, and seeing what a fright they looked, they began to laugh. Benny, who was usually so pristine perfect, was now pinto or an appaloosa, with dark patches and dark spots! Hoot had a black eye and sooty wing tips that looked like boxing gloves, and sooty, black stained feet. The snails, poor chaps, would look dry and charred for at least several days. It was just as well they were all able to laugh, for although they'd escaped evil and horror, they still had a very long way to go.

'Thank you good friends,' began Benny, 'from the deepest places in my heart. What wonderful friends you truly are! I might have fought and won, eventually, but I'll never really know. Your help was timely and extremely brave, and I don't know about all of you, but I've learnt an awful lot. I now know all sorts of things that I didn't understand, and the thing that I know most of all is that Candela and Coraggio picked the very best friends for me!'

Hoot blinked shyly, grateful that they were safe. For several moments Bobs stopped being haughty, and humbly bowed his head. Bibs, young, silly brave chap, blushed bright red at Benny's praise and then, exhausted and sore and chaffed all over, he lay his body gently down and promptly fell asleep.

'I think he's earned his rest, for sure,' smiled Benny.

The others nodded affectionately and agreed.

The group rested then, in the hollow of the hill, while Hoot perched on a high tree branch and took watch. Pleasantly surprised, he saw the piping faun go by, making music that bounced around them. And so it was that even Hoot gave up his fight against sleep and began to doze. He knew enough to understand that where the piping faun was, the sorcerer would never dare to follow.

On and on the music played, in a soothing melody, until the faun merged back into the trees.

CHAPTER 9

Rielle

'Benny, Benny, are you here?' Rielle stopped running. Quickly, she checked over her shoulder. In the silent halls of the Tower of Dreams her shouts and calls bounced loudly off the walls.

Benny... Benny... Benny... Are you... Are you... Here... Here... Here... It went on like that for what seemed like ages.

Shuddering, Rielle swirled around. 'I have to shut the doors,' she shouted to Pud, 'in case that snake comes after us!' Fearfully and reluctantly, she turned and ran back to the entrance of the tower.

'There's no door,' she gasped, realising why it was so easy for her to run inside, 'just the opening onto the bridge. Oh Pud,' she breathed, alarmed, as she peeked outside, 'in all the stories I've heard about fortresses, there's always been a huge door to block the entrance!' She checked the landscape for signs of the snake, but instead, splendid almond trees in blossom greeted her eyes. Hesitantly, Rielle looked back into the tower.

'Keep watch, Pud,' she begged, 'in case that creature catches up. Hooley bondooley, I don't want to think about it.' She braced her shoulders. 'Quickly,' she whispered, 'there must be someone in this place who can help and protect us from that... that beast!'

Solemnly, they crossed a space of intricate floor covered in strange foreign symbols and colourful designs. Walking from one chamber to another, Rielle grew tired of the echoes of their footfalls and also from constantly peering over her shoulder. She stopped and peered upward.

'So, this is the fabled Tower of Dreams,' she grumbled. 'It looked small from the hilltop, but it's enormous now we're inside.'

The roof channelled off into overwhelming regions so high that the ceiling was lost in dark, distant shadows. Arched windows that looked as if giants had built them embraced the walls like silent keepers. Streams of sunlight peered in to shyly caress the infinite stone floors. Columns arose from those same floors, reaching to the ceilings for solace and support. Designs spread delicately underfoot in fantastic patterns that were almost mesmerising.

It wasn't what Rielle had expected. In fact, she wasn't sure what she had expected. She always thought that she would like the tower, but now that she was here, she wasn't so sure. There were statues scattered around and they were terribly life-like. Rielle avoided them where she could.

'Well,' she mumbled as they strode on, 'this is where Hope lives, eh? Let's just see then, shall we?' She walked on with speedy purpose, as floating bits of obstinacy rose up within her.

'How hard can it be to find Hope?' Rielle muttered, dismayed by the small sound of her voice. She shivered. 'Look at all these statues, Pud. It's almost as if they're real.'

Pud padded on undisturbed. It was true, though. The statues looked like they were ready to move. Some were of people going about their business, dressed in costumes that were unusual, and some were of strange animals and unknown creatures. They all seemed to stare with lifelike eyes, but Rielle could have sworn that if she'd asked them they would have come alive. Hushed, somewhere in the distance, someone was speaking. Rielle listened carefully. It wasn't just one voice. It was like the rustling of a million whispers.

'I don't like it here, Pud,' she breathed. 'Let's keep moving, shall we? There must be someone we can speak to soon.' She checked over her shoulder. The snake was nowhere in sight. Timidly, she tried to avoid the statues and their watching eyes as she crept on through the halls. Pud was behaving strangely again. He was looking at the statues in a friendly kind of way.

'They aren't real, Pud,' Rielle stuttered nervously, not believing it even as she said it. Frozen eyes stared at her. Limbs of stone seemed ready to stir. Rielle looked at the floor and hurried on. Panic was fluttering inside her chest.

'Hello?' she called from time to time. 'Hello? Is anyone here?'

The halls echoed and still no one came. The tower seemed empty.

'I... I'm looking for Hope,' Rielle called out softly. 'Is there someone who can tell Hope I'm here?'

*I... I... I... looking... looking... looking... for... for... for...
Hope... Hope... Hope...*

Rielle caught a sob in her throat. This was a terrible and frightening place! It was nothing at all like she thought it would be! Statues brushed against her clothes as something wispy sped past her face and a breeze chilled her skin and hands. Without thinking, she began to jog and then to run. Finally she bolted as fast as she could. She couldn't be near the statues any more! She didn't know where she was heading, but she knew she couldn't stay inside the tower.

Bewildered, Pud followed. He'd been staring keenly at a group of statues, almost as if he were having a chat.

'Maybe, Pud,' Rielle panted, 'if we run enough, we'll bump into Benny and the others.' With a surge of relief, Rielle escaped the tower through wide open back doors. Hurtling outside, she leapt the bank of the little moat, revelling in the slap of the sun's warming heat. Birds whistled, elfin-like, in trees that reached out to her. Fragrant spent blossom and almond nuts charmed the ground. Rielle laughed, relieved.

'This must be the garden to the Tower of Dreams,' she chuckled, as the orchard beamed at her with its tranquil, sweet face. It was lovely! She felt a bit ashamed. Now that she was outside in this beautiful place, she wondered why she'd been so scared. She forced herself to look back at the tower. There was something moving inside! Swift shadows passed by the windows. Who was it? There'd been no one there just moments ago.

'I'm not going back in there to find out,' she hissed. 'I

hate this place, Pud!' She clenched frightened teeth, but then became distracted.

With a quiet, delicate stride, an old man walked slowly by in the garden. Flowing from his ancient chin was a long, grey beard that matched, in colour, the soft stuff of his hood and robe.

Rielle could have shouted with relief. 'At last, Pud,' she grinned. 'Oh Pud, this could be Hope. Hello there! Hello!' she called out.

With a measured look, the old man turned to face her.

'Do you know Hope?' Rielle asked eagerly. A stab of sunlight pierced her eyes and pain flickered through her head. Stopping short, she put a hand to her brow. Her star-scar was hot.

Pud stepped gingerly and looked up at his mistress with a worried frown. He whined anxiously. She looked unwell.

'Did you say you're looking for Hope?' the old man asked, breaking the moment with a soft, soothing voice.

'Ah, yes,' breathed Rielle, 'I'm looking for Hope.' She paused and still holding her brow, she leaned on Pud. Her head felt fit to crack. 'I've been hungry and tired, and, well, busy lately. I suppose these things just catch up.'

She looked at the old man as his knowing eyes gazed softly into hers. 'I'm sorry,' she explained. 'I think the tower made me unwell.'

The old man nodded. 'Well then, that explains it,' he chuckled, and with a wizened, weak hand, he gently took her arm.

Pud growled.

'Shush, silly Pud,' Rielle scolded.

The old man chuckled sweetly at Pud. 'Isn't he a good, protective dog then?' he crooned. 'Nice dog, nice dog,' he whispered.

Pud shrank back with a sullen eye.

'Silly boy,' Rielle murmured. 'It's alright now, Pud.'

'Let's get you something to eat then, young miss, and maybe we can make your headache go away.' The old man smiled at Rielle but she didn't see it. Her head had started to ache in earnest.

'Are you Hope?' Rielle asked. 'I followed my friends here to find Hope. Have you seen them?' She rattled on. 'There was no one in the tower. You have no idea how happy I am we've found you.' She tried to smile, despite her headache.

'There, there,' The old man crooned, 'don't rile yourself about that silly tower. I'm here now, and you were right, Hope lives here, don't you worry.'

Rielle sighed with relief. They were in the right place!

'Oh thank goodness,' she breathed. 'I was right after all. There was no need for Benny and the others to come to Wish for me.'

Pud walked stiff-limbed beside Rielle.

'Benny?' The old man peered at Rielle. 'He's obviously a little friend of yours,' he queried, as his bushy eyebrows jiggled playfully. 'And who are the others?'

Almost forgetting her headache, Rielle felt a rush of heart-glowing warmth. 'Yes,' she beamed. 'Benny, he's... well, he's a wonderful friend, even though I haven't known him long.'

Pud yipped.

'Hush, Pud,' Rielle cautioned. 'My friend Benny,' she continued with heartfelt pride, 'is a little unicorn!'

The old man looked deeply into her eyes as Pud wrestled on the grass with something unseen.

'A little unicorn, eh,' the old man chuckled. 'Well, fancy that. How wonderful!'

Pud yipped once more and walked in front of Rielle.

'Be careful, Pud,' she scolded, 'or I'll trip over.'

The old man smiled and he gripped her arm tightly. 'It's such a comfort,' he sighed feebly, 'to be able to hold onto someone as I walk. To be old is a sad thing, my dear. I think I will need to get myself a walking staff.'

'I'm glad I can help,' Rielle murmured, but where he held her arm, it was beginning to hurt. 'Are we close to Hope yet?' she queried with her star-scar on fire. She was keener than ever to find Benny.

The old man cackled, startling her. 'You'll never find Hope now, young miss,' he spat.

Distressed, Rielle looked up. Gone was his meek expression. Instead, he glowered and seethed at her with a strange unexplained rage. Frightened, Rielle struggled, but he held on tightly, chuckling hideously at some private joke.

'Who are you?' Rielle pleaded. 'Please let me go! What have I done? What have I said?' The old man chortled loudly, dragging her powerfully by the arm.

Rielle resisted, but his grip was increasingly strong. Her head throbbed so piercingly that she thought her skull would crack. She placed her free hand onto her forehead again and a powerful picture of the herd came into her mind. *Now you belong,* she had been told. It was then that Rielle knew this was no ordinary headache.

'You aren't Hope!' Rielle cried, as she fought and struggled. 'Let me go, let me go, let me go!'

But the old man laughed. 'You'll do just fine as my little prisoner,' he cackled. 'You'll be a perfect trap to catch the unicorn!'

'Pud, help me! Help me Pud!' squealed Rielle, but Pud writhed on the grass under a spell.

The Sorcerer of Great Contempt hissed in triumph. 'What a wonderful, unexpected bonus you've turned out to be, young miss. There I was wondering how to trap the unicorn, and out of the amazing blue,' he gestured mockingly as he bowed at the tranquil day, 'you show up!' He roared with such cruel laughter that it simmered in the air.

Pud had known something was wrong. He had never known his mistress to have a headache before, and in his honest dog's heart, he'd known that the meek old man was not nice at all! Determined to make his mistress see the truth, he'd been cut down by the sorcerer in a secret, knowing curse. Pud struggled as Rielle cried out in fear, but the spell was binding.

Then Pud remembered something! In the glade that very night, he and Candela had exchanged some thoughts.

'Whether Rielle does right or wrong,' Candela's unspoken thoughts had been, 'you will guard and protect her through thick and thin, even if it means that your own life is imperilled. That is your lot, faithful Pud.'

Candela had placed white mist from the Ritual of Return over Pud to make him stronger, just in case. *'Go forth now, you faithful dog. Your mistress needs you, no matter what.'*

The white unicorn-mist now unravelled from Pud's heart, and mixed with his true love and unyielding faithfulness, it cracked the sorcerer's spell, freeing Pud to move.

Rielle was almost out of sight as the sorcerer dragged her, struggling, calling, punching and kicking, but it did no good against his strength.

Fury seeped through Pud's bones. His mistress' screams for help made his fur stand on end. Hot rage rippled through his blood, as frenzy muddied the taste in his mouth. Unrestrained daring became his accomplice, and his once gentle eyes became the eyes of a fiend.

Pud crept with cunning and sly creeping stealth, stalking the sorcerer so that he could save Rielle. Slathering and wolf-like, he trailed his prey, as with ballerina feet he tip-toed with speed. Slinking soundlessly, he caught up to them. Pud leapt then, without a thought for himself.

In that moment, Rielle turned around and she didn't recognise her faithful friend. For one split moment Pud was more fearsome than the old man or the snake! With his hackles raised and his lips bared wide, his teeth exposed and a maddened eye, this was not the simple Pud that Rielle knew.

Pud leapt high with unicorns in his heart, landing like the unleashed furies on the sorcerer's back. Blinded by rage with his huge teeth poised, Pud bit hard and wouldn't let go. Gone was the playful Pud, the happy dog who sneezed with joy. Gone was the Pud who hid his face and placed his paws onto Rielle's shoes. Pud bit the Sorcerer of Great Contempt. He didn't know where, he just knew that he did.

Roaring with surprise and pain, the sorcerer fell, letting go of Rielle's arm.

Spitting a mouthful of vile-tasting clothes, Pud leapt away with relief. He looked for his mistress then, and gently, as though she were a new born lamb, he took Rielle's hand in his lips. Almost with an apology, Pud urged her to run.

Although Candela despised rage and carnage, she would have been proud of the dog in that moment.

They ran and ran and didn't stop. Sweet blossom petals brushed them on their final falling to the ground, and birds trilled and called, urging them on. At last, Rielle and Pud found a little cave where they could hide. With a quick look behind them, they scuttled into its shelter. The cave was just big enough for Rielle to stand. Sunlight dribbled like a thread through a small hole in the cave roof, shedding some light and warmth.

Rielle looked at Pud with relief. He was *her* Pud again. For a heartbeat, however, she was almost afraid of him. She'd never seen him like that. She looked down to where he lay with his worried eyes fixed on the cave's entrance. As if sensing her thoughts, Pud looked back at his mistress and whined softly in his throat.

Rielle let go of her misgivings and hugged him hard. 'You saved my life, my dear, true friend,' she gasped. 'Oh,

Pud, you'd never abandon me and leave me all alone! You'd never leave me to face danger or harm.' A shadow crossed Rielle's face. This journey to Wish was nothing like she had thought it would be.

She slumped against the brown back wall of the cave. She was tired of chasing or being chased. 'I hate this journey we're on. I hate this stupid quest! It's been nothing but hardship, and now look at all this trouble we're in.'

She hugged her dog harder. 'I'm so sorry, Pud. All of this is my fault. We should have stopped wandering long ago and then none of this would ever have happened!' The shadow in her eyes deepened. 'I knew I wouldn't find Hope. I knew Hope wouldn't be there, but it doesn't matter, Pud, because there are other things I can do in Wish!'

Pud sat up. He looked sincerely into Rielle's eyes and his heart grew cold. She was going to do something rash; he could feel it. Candela had warned him that this moment might come. Pud jumped to his feet and nudged Rielle hard.

'Why should I keep looking for what I've lost?' Rielle scowled.

Pud began to whine.

Rielle took a deep, ragged breath. 'Look at all the danger we've been through, just because of... of something that happened long ago!' Rielle barely noticed that Pud was making all sorts of sounds. The star-scar on her brow was red and hot as she let anger burn through her.

'I wish,' Rielle began, as Pud barked in her face, 'I

wish with all my heart.... ' She faltered as if her heart understood, and battled with legions to stop the thought. 'I wish,' she began again, 'that the reason for my stupid quest, the reason I've wandered, searching all this time....' Rielle's intensity gathered as she spoke. 'I wish....'

A noise interrupted her. Pud stopped barking and slumped with relief. Rielle turned to the cave's entrance.

'Uh, uh, uh! Stop right there, young lady!'

Rielle didn't just stop; she jumped a foot in the air. There, at the entrance of their hideaway, was the enormous snake!

Oobaat peered good-naturedly at Rielle but obviously he wasn't welcome.

'If I ever have to do this shape changing thing again,' he muttered despairingly under his breath, *'I should pick something cute and cuddly, but what can one do when one is in a hurry?'*

Oobaat sighed aloud. 'Oh for goodness sake and for all the beasts in every kingdom,' he cried at Rielle's terrified expression, 'don't worry, don't worry. For goodness ssssake, I'm not going to eat you!'

'Hooley dooley, do something Pud,' Rielle whispered. But Pud just sat and watched.

Oobaat moved closer. Rielle stifled a scream. She pushed herself harder into the cave's back wall, but there was nowhere left to go.

'You're jumping to conclusions,' continued the gatekeeper. 'You don't know who I am or what it is I'm here for. You haven't the faintest idea whether I'm a friend or foe, but you've decided, haven't you, that I have bad intentions?' Oobaat pushed his large head even closer to Rielle, where she sat round-eyed in horror, too scared to breathe.

Stay calm, she kept thinking to herself. *Stay calm and think of a way out.*

But Oobaat interrupted her thoughts with a loud hiss. Blinking his slanting yellow eyes, he went on abruptly. 'I have a motto, and it goes precisely like this.' He cleared his throat as if this was something that he'd rehearsed.

When in doubt don't rush
When insecure don't conclude
Don't speak before you think
And when unsure don't assume
Oh, and most importantly of all, stay away from weak-willed friends!

Oobaat looked shrewdly at Rielle and Pud, as his long orange tongue poked the air. 'If you want a road map to life, all you need is those five things. Otherwise all your little fears and doubts will jump and itch like fleas in your mind!' He paused. 'Much like I imagine they're doing right now?' He stopped to guess the result of his words. 'Mind you,' he continued to the dumbstruck Rielle, 'all of the above may take years of practise, and a great long time to perfect.'

Oobaat sat back and let curiosity do its job. *Humans,* he thought. *What an awful lot of effort they are!* He watched Rielle silently. It worked. His stillness succeeded where his chatter had failed.

'Who… who are you?' Rielle finally croaked. 'What do you want? Why are you chasing us?' She clung closely to Pud. She was still working on a plan of escape.

'For goodness sake,' Oobaat said in a rush, as his yellow eyes flashed and his thick neck grew flat, 'get over the idea that I'm going to bite!'

Rielle squealed at his sharp retort and flattened herself onto the cave's wall.

Oobaat, old friend, the gatekeeper mused, *you've got to look meek and mild. You've frightened the girl even more. What a pity she can't see me as I really am!* He tried again in a sweeter tone.

'I implore you not to be afraid. I'm not who you think I am. Truly! My name is Oobaat and I'm a keeper of records. I guard a wishing gate. The one you came through, as a matter of fact. I'm here to help you, I promise, young lady.'

Rielle shook her head. It didn't really make sense. 'Why should I need your help?' she whispered. But before Oobaat could answer, she stuttered on. 'Just a minute, do you mean you… you're like that frog we met at the pond?'

Oobaat grimaced. 'Ahh, yes, that frog,' he replied, but quickly changed tack and continued on. 'Yes, as a matter of fact, that's *my* job. I record who's passing through to Wish and I also record the reason for their vissssit.' He rolled his eyes. Sometimes he just couldn't help talking in snake.

'You see,' Oobaat explained, 'in case you didn't know, Wish is made from the minds of humans and things promptly come and go. It's not enough to write your names on lily pads, I must also record why you're passing through.'

'I already told the frog.' Rielle didn't believe him. Oobaat could see it in her eyes. 'So,' Rielle continued, 'why should I tell you?'

Oobaat was stumped. Why indeed? How could he prove who he was? All Rielle was seeing, after all, was a huge green snake who could talk!

'Why should I tell you?' she snapped again. 'As far as I know, you're some enormous horrible creature that's part of this miserable, uncomfortable land and any minute you'll just decide to eat us and no one will find us again.'

'Ahhh, I think I see now.' Oobaat almost smiled. 'You must be the girl that young Benny wants to help.'

Rielle gasped and, despite herself, her eyes lit up. 'You know Benny?' she cried.

'Yes,' Oobaat stated.

'How do you know Benny?' Rielle persisted. 'Or is he sitting in your stomach as one of your meals?' She cast a knowing look at Oobaat's large girth.

'Be still, young lady!' Oobaat bellowed. 'Benny the little unicorn has come to this infernal place because he wanted to find Hope and give you a gift! Even as we speak, he walks with danger and it's all because he felt you were worth it.'

Oobaat dropped his snake head to the ground, and with an effort, he turned sadly and began to leave the cave.

Pud barked and ran after him.

'It's no use, faithful dog,' Oobaat sighed. 'Perhaps your mistress is a hopeless case.'

But Pud circled in front of him, doing his best to block the cave's entrance.

Rielle felt sudden shame. If she thought about it, it was obvious that if the snake had planned to eat them, it would already have done so. Besides, he seemed to know all about Benny and his reason for being in Wish. She looked cautiously at him. Now he was leaving in anger. After the horrible old man, it was hard to trust anybody, but everything that Oobaat said made sense. Could he be telling the truth? She *had* thought Rana was shifty at the time. Maybe Oobaat really was the keeper to the wishing pond. She sure could use some help right now!

'Don't go!' she called. 'I... I'll tell you why I came to Wish.'

Oobaat turned back. His ploy had worked very well indeed! He fixed her with his yellow eyes and waited.

'I came here to find my unicorn friend,' Rielle began, 'and, and I suppose I also wanted to find the Tower of Dreams. You know, to see Hope. So you can write that down in your record book.'

'Are you sssure?' Oobaat asked. He held her with a gentle but knowing look. He sighed. *Give me patience in this moment.*

'What do you mean, am I sure?' Rielle countered.

'Are you sure that is your true reason for coming to Wish?' Oobaat hissed. *Sometimes being a gatekeeper and having to record things was something of a chore!*

Rielle blushed at the intensity of his gaze.

'Come on, young lady,' Oobaat urged, 'we all have choices to make,' he insisted. 'Which ones are yourssss?' Oobaat stared hard, making his eyes probing and sharp.

'I came here to find Hope,' Rielle scowled, 'but there was nothing at all in that silly tower, just a bunch of stupid statues!'

She sighed. She knew she would have to tell the truth. There was nowhere else that she could run right now, not with Oobaat blocking the cave. He looked stubborn. He might keep them there for a very long time.

'All right,' she exclaimed, 'all right then. Do you want me to be truly honest?'

Oobaat nodded, but then, before Rielle and Pud's bewildered eyes, he began to bob his head and hiss:

The truth
Is neither lost
Nor something we discover
It simply sits
And waits for us
Quietly under cover

Some do say
The truth will hurt
Yet others will chatter
White lies are good
So in the grand scheme of things
Does it really matter?

Let me see
Why did you say it's half past three
When in fact
It's five past four

Tell me true
What say you?

Nothing serious did I intend
It can't hurt me
It can't hurt you
Too much energy you expend
On little words
So why make such a bother?

Is that a lie?
May I ask why?
Now look at that
Have missed my bus
And goodness knows
Will there be another?

Where are you going?
You can't stop now?
No time to talk?
You missed the bus?
A hundred miles
You must now walk...

A tiny joke
If not for me
Has cost you greatly
And dearly
Your journey is now ten times three
I didn't think, I didn't see.

Oobaat stopped and waited quietly.

Rielle nodded. 'I... I wanted to put an end to my search, my quest,' she began in a small, downcast voice. 'I wanted to stop being unhappy and sad.' She looked up defiantly. 'I wanted to believe that there was a way to do that, and then Benny said that Wish can make things happen for humans.' Rielle glared. 'I wanted my unhappiness to go away.' She gulped. 'Is that so big a thing to ask?'

Oobaat moved closer. 'At what cost, Rielle?' he prompted quietly.

Rielle looked him squarely in the eyes. 'I'm not a bad person,' she replied. 'I just wanted my life to become good, that's all.'

Oobaat settled himself more comfortably. 'Tell me,' he coaxed, 'tell me what you're hiding from the world.'

Pud yipped.

Rielle knew that this time she would have to tell him. She sighed and slumped by the cave's brown wall.

'I lived like other people once,' she began. 'I had a family and even a bedroom of my own. I was happy, just like other people are.' She paused, and remembered herself in a wonderful garden, dancing and laughing and playing games.

'One day, my parents went away. I missed them, but I knew they'd come home. I stayed with my uncle and aunt.' Suddenly Rielle couldn't talk fast enough. 'I thought I would always have my parents, but I was wrong, old snake.' She glared at Oobaat, anger clouding her brow. 'I was wrong!'

'Aunt was kind and so was uncle, but it wasn't really the same. They told me my Dad got a new job. They said it took him and my mother away from home and kept them busy all the time.' Rielle frowned and her eyes became fierce, but she carried on. 'I kept asking my aunt why they'd been gone for so long, but all she told me was that they were very busy and didn't have much time.'

Rielle stammered on. 'I... I often wondered if they stayed away so long because of something that I had done. I tried doing lots of nice things to make them notice me, but they just got busier and busier and were hardly ever home. In the end, they had no time for me at all. It was as if I had just disappeared!'

Oobaat sat up. He sensed that the important part was still to come.

Rielle held Pud hard now and her breath came fast. Pud quickly placed his paw on her shoe, then licked her ear and whined gently in his throat.

'One day,' Rielle barely whispered, 'one day,' she gulped, 'my parents left me a note.' She smiled ruefully. 'A note! Who leaves a note for a little girl?'

Oobaat swallowed a lump in his throat.

Rielle continued. 'The note said: *We are going away for a long while but you can stay with uncle and aunt.*' Rielle looked up with her eyes ablaze. 'That's all. That's all that was written. They didn't even sign it *with love from Mum and Dad!*'

Suddenly her eyes misted and her voice went small. 'I've always wondered what I did that was bad. It had to be my fault, didn't it? They simply went away.'

Oobaat sighed. 'So what happened when your parents returned?'

'They never did return!' Rielle exploded.

Oobaat pondered. 'Did you think perhaps,' he began, 'that something might have, er, happened to them so that they couldn't return?'

'Oh, did I think that!' Rielle burst out. 'I made up long, sad stories in my imagination. I had every reason in the world worked out why they didn't come home! For two years I imagined that I rescued my parents from savage tribes, wild animals and from unknown places and frightful diseases! But then it came one day.' She stalled and looked up. 'A letter. From them. It came with another note for me. The letter said that they would return when they could, but there were things that they had to take care of first. That's all. No proper explanation. The note went on to say that in the meantime, I'd be well cared for. That's all they wrote and there was nothing else. They didn't even believe I was smart enough to understand, or that I needed to know why.'

Rielle was talking fast and clipping her words. 'I remember people fussed over me. They were kind and caring and I'm grateful for that, but I waited and kept telling myself that it was all a mistake and that they'd soon come home.' Her voice drifted.

'I waited. Every day I wished they would get back. Soon... I would tell myself... soon. But the months passed and then a year went by, and no one would really talk about it much or tell me what was going on.' She shrugged. 'Do people think children are stupid or something? Don't they understand that we have a right to know things too?'

Oobaat nodded and Rielle calmed down.

'Finally, one day I asked my best friend, but she didn't know anything, and my aunt and uncle would just say stuff that sounded nice but was altogether useless.' Rielle took a deep breath and new fire leapt into her eyes.

'Then one night I knew I had to find out for myself!' Her eyes flashed. 'I jumped out of bed and changed my clothes. I took the money I'd saved from doing chores and I stuffed a bag with things I'd need. Then I ran next door to say goodbye to my oldest friend.' Her voice became hoarse. 'My friend was anxious at first but then she was sad, and instead of telling me I was only a girl, she gave me her favourite hat.' Rielle stroked the blue hat in her hand. 'I told her I was going to find Mother and Dad. Of course she thought I should wait at home, but she knew me well enough to know I'd made up my mind. She wished me luck, even though she thought I should stay.'

Rielle held Pud closer. 'I had an address, on an old letter, of one of the places they had been and I went to find it.' She paused quietly then looked down. 'They weren't there, but the people were kind and they gave me another address. My parents weren't there either. I tried to find where they'd gone after that but no one knew, and so I thought perhaps I would go home.' She looked up at Oobaat imploringly. 'I... well, something happened then, and I changed my mind. I think that was when I just gave up. You know? I kept on walking after that, just kept on going. It seemed the easiest thing to do.'

Rielle sighed raggedly as tears caught in her throat. 'I've been wandering ever since. I realise now there's no way I'll find my parents, but at least I've become good at wandering. It's my life now. When I really think about it, I made a decision that day. I decided that I no longer wanted to find someone who had left me behind!'

'You wouldn't go back?' asked Oobaat. 'You know, just in case your parents have returned?'

Rielle scowled. 'I told you, this is my life now; it's what I do! Besides, why shouldn't my parents suffer, just like I have? I'm not that little girl that went searching anymore.' She swallowed in fear at having said it aloud.

She looked openly at Oobaat. 'I want you to believe me! Maybe you can understand that when I heard Wish existed, well, it was my chance, don't you see? I know it's hard after what you've heard, but I did come to Wish to try to make things right somehow. '

Oobaat nodded wisely. He didn't like Wish. He'd been a gatekeeper for aeons of time and yet the task didn't seem to get any easier. It was moments like these that made it terribly complicated. Of course, it was all about the record books; they demanded that these things be written down. That was his job. It seemed simple but in truth it was so very difficult.

'Are you afraid?' he asked.

Rielle took a deep breath. 'No, I'm not afraid any more,' she replied, 'but sometimes I'm angry. I'm angry and hurt but mostly sad.'

Oobaat pushed her harder. 'Do you really believe it's

your fault that they left you, well... behind?'

Rielle looked at Oobaat and pleaded. 'I don't know! I mean, I tried so hard to be a good little girl! Oh snake, I thought time was meant to heal all wounds, but it hasn't for me. No matter where I wander or how far I go, I still hurt and I still feel the pain.'

Oobaat raised his thick snake neck until it did a kind of dance. *I know it's not my place to give advice,* he thought, *oh, but what the heck, I can only get fired from this confounded job!*

'Tut, tut, young thing,' he quipped, 'time doesn't heal your heart, my dear; all time does is lend a distance. It isn't time that heals your wounds; pain is healed by love and kindness. What you really must remember is that sometimes you have to try and trust, if not others, than at least yourself.' He gazed at Rielle with wonderfully gentle eyes.

'It wasn't your fault things went wrong, young lady. You were just a child; remember that always. Your pain may stay with you and that's the truth, but there's a little unicorn out there seeking Hope for you, and that is something very special. It means you're loved and dearly blessed.' Oobaat felt his big heart break as he watched the young girl battle with her sadness. 'I'm sure your parents love you in their own way,' he whispered. But he could see that Rielle wasn't listening.

'Do you see that's why I knew I had to go?' Rielle implored. 'Why I knew I had to go on my journey? I thought if I searched for long enough perhaps I would find them, and ask what was wrong.' She sighed. 'After I got lost, I didn't know where I was going, of course, but I wandered along the road for a while eating berries and things, and I drank from streams.' She looked up at Oobaat, surprising him with something like a smile.

'Then one day... I'd lost track of time.' Rielle stroked Pud's head and her voice grew soft. 'One day... I saw a tiny puppy whimpering in some bushes, and I knew that just like me, he had no one.' She hugged Pud as he nudged her hard. 'It was then that I knew I'd have to be strong, because I had a small friend to take care of as well.'

Rielle blinked away tears as she looked into Oobaat's kind eyes. 'I wanted, just now... I was going to wish for my parents to die!' She covered her face with her hands and paused while demons held her heart. Then she looked imploringly up at the snake.

'Why did they leave me? They were supposed to take care of me. After all, I was just a little girl! They left me and didn't look back once. They... they didn't even say a proper goodbye. They left me, and I had no one to truly call my own.'

Oobaat recoiled at her haunted face. 'Yes,' he replied, nodding slowly. 'Yes, I understand. But if you throw a ball against a wall, then you'd better be prepared to catch it when it returns.'

Surprised, Rielle realised that she no longer feared the snake.

'What do you mean?' she demanded.

'What I mean,' Oobaat replied, choosing his words with care, 'is that there is no such thing as us and them; the way we treat everything counts, even if it's a rock or a little bird. What you wish for others, Rielle, will eventually come back to be with you.'

'Even if it's someone horrible, who's hurt you?' Rielle shouted as she stood up furiously.

Oobaat knew she wasn't a bad person. He understood that she was hurt and angry. 'When people are selfish or thoughtless or cruel,' he replied carefully, 'it's because they tell lies, mostly to themselves, and because they live in fear to be brave or true. One day, some way, your parents will know what they've done.'

'But will they pay?' Rielle sobbed.

Oobaat looked pensive before he answered. 'Would you be them?' he asked.

Rielle stopped crying and looked up. She looked deep into the snake's slanted yellow eyes. She looked at Pud who was tilting his head.

'No,' she replied at last, in a hushed tone. 'No, I wouldn't be them for all the wishes in the world.'

Oobaat waited. 'I think we should go back now,' he eventually whispered. 'Wish is not the place for you, so why don't you let Benny find Hope instead?'

Rielle looked at the snake with wonder. 'That's exactly what Candela told me I should do.'

'Then follow me,' called Oobaat. 'Follow me and I'll show you the way back.' He shouted with cheer and enormous relief!

Rielle hesitated for a moment.

'For goodness sake and for all the beasts in every kingdom,' cried Oobaat, 'don't worry, don't worry, I'm still not going to eat you!'

It was Pud who took charge. Knowing that the forest

was the best place to be, he left Rielle gawping and began racing after the gatekeeper.

'Wait for me!' called Rielle, as she quickly gave chase.

Oobaat led them over the brow of the hill and there, just below them, were the shores of Wish. 'Come on!' he called.

He plunged into the water and once again became a tortoise! Holding their breath, with eyes shut tightly, Pud dove in and so did Rielle!

CHAPTER 10

High Hope

'We must continue,' yawned Benny, as he woke from a fitful doze and scrambled to his feet. Bibs nodded and put on a brave face, but Bobs looked old and tired.

Hoot had flown ahead. 'Look!' he called. He was pointing to something in the distance.

Benny found the strength to jog. Poor, charred Bibs and Bobs slid up the hill as best they could. Without much cheer, they all looked to where Hoot was pointing. Hugged by wisps of tattered cloud, there stood a range of purple mountains. Just as legend told, and somewhat to the right, in a forest of flowering trees, there nestled a fortress.

'That must be the Tower of Dreams,' breathed Hoot.

'It is,' whispered Bobs. 'I remember how it looked.'

'It's splendid!' exclaimed Benny, laughing aloud.

'It really does exist,' smiled Bibs, forgetting his bruises for the moment.

'Of course it does,' snorted Bobs. But he looked at Bibs almost kindly. Things had changed somehow, since the battle.

Seeing the Tower of Dreams in the distance gave them all a surge of strength. With new spirit and expectation, they quickly moved down the hill without another word.

The way was rocky and risky. Boulders and pebbles crumbled and fell around their feet. They had to be cautious so as not to lose their footing, or they could plunge to the bottom below. It sorely tested them after all they'd been through, but finally, they reached the valley floor.

Forests of almond trees in full flower swayed gently in the breeze, murmuring with the sound of easy-growing things. Almond tree branches brushed the group as they passed. The ground was charmingly covered in a carpet of fallen pink and white blossom. Birds hopped from welcoming tree branches as small creatures went about their daily chores. Young almond trees grew at the knees of the old. Nuts still in their shells littered the ground, making a crunching sound when Benny stepped on them. Creamy oils spilled out from those nuts and as the snails slid over them, they found that their bellies were being greased, which was a mighty relief for their sore, burnt bits.

'Thank you,' whispered Benny to no one in particular. Smiling with satisfaction, he turned to the others. 'This is it,' he beamed. 'There's no time like the present, so let's go!' With a huge buck of joy, Benny went from a standstill to a flat-out gallop. With his mane and tail flying, his hooves struck sparks on the ground.

'After you,' gestured Hoot to the snails, with an out-flung wing.

Not to be outdone by Benny's speed, the others bolted after him with a cheer. Down petal-strewn paddocks the four travellers sped, up one hill and then down into the Valley of Possibility. There it was: the Tower of Dreams!

The group reached the banks of the moat when Benny propped. He looked around at the others and saw that their faces mirrored his own. With mixed feelings, the group stilled their thoughts and calmed their minds. This was it! Inside that building might be what they were seeking. Would they find Hope? Would Hope have an answer? Did Rielle have a dream? No one moved. Together, the small band of trusty friends stood, and in the hush they let it sink in.

'Here we are,' whispered Benny, 'we're really here, everyone. Any minute now we might find Hope.'

Surrounding the tower, the trees were stooped, wise and proud. They watched the travellers as trees will do, then shed more blossoms onto the ground. The small moat lulled sleepily, with just the little wooden bridge for them to cross. Time stood still.

Benny breathed in before choosing his moment. Bobs and Bibs peeked up from either side of his legs as Hoot rode a current of wind.

I have to go in now, thought Benny. His decision made, he placed his first hoof upon the bridge and, with tiptoe steps, he walked on. His hooves sounded clip-clop on the bridge. He looked about as he went, with his neck arched and his ears fully forward. No pain came from his horn, so it seemed that all was well.

Hoot dropped to Benny's height and took his place to

Benny's right and then with his huge night eyes agog, he flew forward, matching Benny's stride.

'Well,' Benny sighed, 'it looks like we're here.'

They all stepped inside. As one, they let out a breath of relief and then looked at each other and sheepishly grinned.

'Everything feels just the same,' whispered Bibs. The others nodded in relief. 'I... I thought it might go clang or something, or there'd be a big welcome mat or people coming to the door to say hello.' Bibs sounded disappointed.

'Yes, the tower does lead you to have some kind of expectation,' agreed Benny. 'However, everything feels the same, and maybe that's just as good.'

'Nothing's changed just because of us,' Hoot sensibly quipped. 'After all, we're just visitors, remember?'

'I wonder where Hope is,' Benny murmured.

The tower was huge. It had rows of crisscrossed archways that reached far into the ceiling. There were diamond-shaped windows made of multi coloured glass and delightful patterns were crafted into the floors.

Busy creatures and beings of every kind were dashing about on all sorts of errands. No one seemed to notice the newcomers much. Chatter filtered cheerily through the air and somewhere music played in a lilting way. Muffled laughter bounced from the ceiling as tower dwellers got on with living.

The travellers walked quietly through the halls, nodding hello, bobbing their heads and bowing politely to anyone they met. Friendly occupants greeted them as if they belonged, and no one seemed surprised to see them, so Benny and the others began to feel almost at home. Occasionally, Benny would stop someone and politely ask if they had seen Hope. But as friendly as everyone was, they would just shake their heads and dash off.

Benny, Hoot, Bibs and Bobs were tired and battle-scarred; they just wanted to find Hope.

Bibs didn't want to admit to the others that deep down, he was afraid that the sorcerer would find them, and that they'd never see the forest again. With some of his old eagerness, Bibs forgot caution and peeked around, poking his nose into empty doorways. He was convinced that if he looked hard enough, then he would be the one to see Hope first. With that thought, he scooted off.

Benny glanced at the others. 'Did you see where Bibs went?' he asked. They shook their heads anxiously as their faces mirrored his concern.

'Bibs?' Benny queried, but there was no answer.

'We're on strange new ground, after all,' Bobs crossly added. 'We need him to behave himself inside the tower.'

'Let's hurry,' Hoot concluded, 'let's hurry before we regret this place.' They picked up speed.

'Bibs, where are you?' Benny called out.

'Do you hear that?' Hoot exclaimed. 'It's someone crying.' They stopped, turning keen ears to listen.

'Bibs!' Benny called again. 'Bibs, where are you?' There was no usual cheery answer.

'Come on.' Benny threw caution to the winds and cantered away. His hooves made a dreadful clatter, but all that mattered was finding Bibs.

They turned into a hallway and there he was, sitting

across from a human figure of startling beauty. She was crying and whispering to Bibs with pleading eyes. Benny and Hoot stepped closer.

'There is no Hope,' she chanted, 'I've looked and looked and Hope isn't here.'

Startled, Benny, Hoot and Bobs glanced at each other. *What was this?*

Bibs watched her in disbelief. Hope had to be here! Otherwise it meant that Candela was wrong. He shuddered. The Tower of Dreams... it sounded like such an easy kind of place, filled with mystery and magic and wonderful things. Surely they should have found Hope by now.

'Who are you?' Bibs whispered, his body quivering with unsettled fear.

'They call me Despair,' she said.

'Despair?' Bibs gaped. 'But we came here to find Hope. This is the Tower of Dreams, isn't it?'

Despair blinked tears at Bibs' innocent face. 'Yes,' she replied, 'this is the Tower of Dreams, but I've searched and searched, and I warn you now that Hope isn't here.'

'But,' stuttered Bibs, 'Hope has to be here, otherwise this entire journey and everything we've done will have been for nothing, and for no good reason!'

Despair put her head into her hands. 'Give up,' she wailed. 'Give up now before the search defeats you.'

Bibs was usually such a happy chap with a big open heart and a smile on his face, but the fight with the sorcerer had left its mark. He was afraid. In a panic, he knew he had to get away. There were tears in Despair's eyes that he couldn't understand. He had to escape from her terrible sadness. Before Benny had a chance to speak, young Bibs turned and blindly bolted.

'No, Bibs, don't run away,' Benny called. But it was too late; Bibs was gone.

'Don't worry, Benny, I'll find him,' Bobs assured, and he too, slid away, as fast as he could.

Benny bunched his body to take up the chase, but with steadfast force, Hoot flew in front of him and held up a wing.

'No, stay, young master; don't sway from your course!' Hoot urged. 'I'll find them and bring them back and we'll all catch up with you soon.'

Benny turned in mid-run. 'But... ' he began.

Hoot stared him piercingly in the eye. 'Remember what we came for,' he declared, 'you mustn't steer from your course. Everything rides on you now. You must go on to look for Hope.'

'But don't you see, Hoot,' Benny cried, 'we've come all this way and been through so much that we can't split up now and risk losing what we've gained.' He blinked. 'Besides, Bibs didn't desert me when I needed help. He risked his life for me, remember?'

'It's my turn to be saying something now,' Hoot replied with dark, cryptic warning. 'This journey is the answer to the conclusion, young Benny. Don't mistake it to be the other way around.'

Benny knew that Hoot was right. If he stopped his search for Hope now, there might not be another chance. He made a decision.

'Promise me, then,' Benny implored, 'promise me with an oath that you will find them both in this mysterious place, and… and that you'll bring us all together as soon as you can. We are on borrowed time here, Hoot. You know, as well as I do, that Wish is not for the likes of us.' He felt as if he were abandoning his crew, especially after all the chances they had taken for him.

'I promise,' Hoot bravely replied, 'on my eyes of night and my wings of flight and all things just and wise.' He tried to laugh but it came out thinly. He tried to joke, but it rang too true. 'Would I risk Candela and Coraggio's anguish, if I didn't return us all safely home?'

The two remaining travellers looked intently at each other then, and Benny knew that Hoot would never give up while he had wisdom in his heart.

'Take care, dear friend,' Benny replied joylessly.

With a resolute nod, brave, good Hoot flew away. 'I've promised, now,' he muttered, 'in this fickle place where there are no guarantees. Ah well, if anyone can find them, it would surely be me.' Into the vast spaces of the tower, prudent Hoot flew to become a small flying speck in the distance.

Benny turned to face Despair, who still wailed and wept.

'Please don't cry. There must be another way,' he gently prodded. 'Hope lives here somewhere, after all.' Despair turned her back to him. With one last look, Benny gave up. His heart knew he could do nothing here. So, alone, he went in search of Hope. Eventually, the sounds of Despair faded away.

Bibs ran with all his might, blinded by the misery of

Despair. On and on through the archways and halls he ran, without thinking or caring where he went.

Bobs followed as quickly as he could after the younger snail, but no matter how hard he chased, he couldn't catch up. He called and called but no one answered and finally, despondent and tired, he slowed down.

'Stupid youngster,' he growled. 'He's a downright pest at the best of times. He decides to run off willy-nilly and then it's up to the rest of us to fix his problem. He's always a nuisance.' Bobs sniffed importantly. 'I don't know what Candela was thinking when she asked him along. He should have stayed in the forest. She should have known that he was nothing but trouble.'

Grumbling, Bobs slid on. A glimmer in the corridor ahead drew him toward a small alcove where a muted light shone. Could Bibs be there? Bobs slid to the alcove, becoming moodier by the moment.

'I want to rest my weary bones. I'm too old and worn out for battles and adventures and senseless brave deeds. I shouldn't have come on this adventure. I can see that now,' Bobs miserably reflected.

Grumbling angrily, he slid right into the alcove. No sooner had he done so than he shrank back. There were bars on the windows and on the doors. It looked like a dungeon. Ice hung from the ceiling and covered the walls. Looking closely, he saw that there was a crumpled figure sitting on the floor.

The figure looked up. 'I've been waiting for you,' it grinned.

Bobs gaped. How grandly and gloriously the figure

was dressed! It wore a jewel-filled crown, a crimson cloak and shoes of gold, but when the figure stood up, Bobs could see that a skeleton lived within the wonderful clothes. Bobs gasped. Surely this wasn't Hope!

'Who are you?' he wheezed, horrified to discover he was trembling.

'I am your friend,' croaked the skeletal face. 'You know me; everyone knows me. I am Hate!'

Then, before Bobs' confused eyes, Hate rushed and shook at the bars. In a fever of torment he tore some down as if the prison repelled him too, but then, as if regretting his actions, he picked up the bars from the floor and tried to put them back. Bobs flinched and turned away. He crawled out of the freezing jail as ice slowly melted from his shell. He felt that the ice would never leave his heart.

Meanwhile, Hoot called for the snails, but receiving no answer, he flew outside in case they'd left the tower. Birds trilled, crickets chirped and the moat lapped against the tower walls.

A cherub sat on the banks of the moat, singing a winsome song. Despite his problems, Hoot smiled. Could this be Hope? He swooped to ask.

'Hope?' Hoot queried, as delight filled his veins. He couldn't wait to tell Benny his news.

'Joy,' answered the cherub with a friendly glance before diving deeply into the water.

Cheered, Hoot flew on. He hadn't found Hope, but Joy still existed, and that made his search suddenly easy.

The ice had melted from Bobs, but he couldn't go on. Grinding to a halt, he saw something ahead.

'Bibs?' he croaked with a parched, dry throat.

Indeed it was Bibs, curled up and fast asleep. Bobs shook his head in familiar annoyance.

'Asleep,' he grumbled. 'Asleep, and all of us worried to death by now. I'll show you sleep, you pain in the neck!'

Bobs slid up to Bibs and bellowed in his ear. 'Wake up, you goof! What was the big idea, running away?' But despite himself, Bobs' heart lit with relief. 'We thought we'd lost you in this great big place,' he muttered gruffly. Bibs opened his eyes. Bobs frowned. 'We're all out looking for you, you nuisance!'

'Hello there, Bobs,' Bibs said, grinning. 'I must say I've missed you. Where are the others?' Bibs looked around. 'Are they here too?'

Bobs sighed. 'Actually, we're lost, but don't worry. I'm sure we'll find them eventually, somehow.' He and Bibs looked shyly at each other.

'Let's go and find Benny, shall we?' urged Bibs.

Benny was missing his friends, but Hoot was right. They had made this journey especially to find Hope. Benny had made a promise to Rielle, and promises were for keeping. Time pressed on. Benny knew that they would have to leave Wish soon.

He trotted and trudged and sometimes galloped, until he thought he'd tried every room and nook of the tower. Some halls were empty but some were filled with life, and although he met all sorts of strangers - some fair, some impressive, some great and some small - none of them answered to the name of Hope. Benny was puzzled. Finally, he stopped. *Don't be discouraged,* he thought to himself; *don't let yourself believe that Despair was right.*

Benny trilled, long and loud, but neither Hoot nor the snails replied.

He shut his eyes and thought of the herd. *What would Candela or Coraggio do,* he wondered, *if they had tried very hard and still had no luck?*

No sooner had the thought taken place than Benny saw the heart-warming herd. In his mind's eye they filled his vision. Benny's heart leapt with joy and new courage.

'Benny dear, when you see Hope, be sure to give my love,' Candela had said.

'Of course,' he exclaimed, 'Candela didn't say *if* you see Hope!' He grinned. 'Candela said *when* you see Hope! So that's it. No one doubts that Hope will be found, so there must be somewhere that I haven't tried. Let me see. I've tried the gardens, I've tried the East wing, West wing, North and South, so where is the one place I've missed or left out?' Then he knew. Much to the amusement of the tower's inhabitants, Benny bolted off.

'This must be it!' Benny careered to a halt. 'We didn't check this one spot when we first came in!' Right inside the entrance to the tower, there was a small hallway. Beyond the hallway there was a room.

'We were so busy looking around when we came in, that we never gave this a second glance.' Benny chuckled. 'Isn't that always the way,' he murmured. 'It so often happens that when we give up, we go last to where we should have gone first!'

He tiptoed through the hallway then peeked inside the room. A figure in a plain brown cloak sat quietly.

'Excuse me please,' whispered tired Benny, 'I was wondering if you might know where Hope could be found?'

Without moving or shifting and in a sober tone, the figure spoke from behind its hood. 'I am the one you're seeking.'

'Hope?' Benny checked, and held his breath.

'Yes, I am Hope.'

'Ahh,' sighed Benny. His heart filled with joy as he wondered why he hadn't found Hope before.

'Hope,' he began shyly, 'I am pleased to meet you. My name is Benny. May I seek permission to ask you a question?'

Hope nodded just once, but it was enough.

Urgently now, for time was short, Benny went on. 'I have a puzzle to ask, please. It's for a friend whose heart is broken and may never mend. She believes that there are no dreams left for her, but I promised I'd find out and bring the answer home.'

At first, Hope said nothing. Then, still seated quietly and without moving, Hope opened a hand, and from it fluttered a small butterfly.

'Yes,' answered Hope, 'yes, young Rielle still has a dream, but she must seek it as it won't come to her.'

'Oh, thank you!' exclaimed a delighted Benny.

'Wait,' spoke Hope, 'I have something for Rielle.' He whispered to the butterfly before releasing her. She flew straight to Benny.

'I give you, in safe keeping,' Hope continued, 'little Far. She is a token for Rielle and also a reminder.' He paused, guardedly. 'Let Rielle know that I wish her well.'

Before Benny had a chance to thank him, Hope went on in a much sterner tone. 'Don't forget, little unicorn, that you must let Rielle know who you really are and promise that before you lend her Far, she will be told the riddle of unicorns!'

'Oh, yes, I'd almost forgotten,' replied Benny. 'Of course I promise. Thank you, Hope, thank you for everything you've done! I can't thank you enough!'

And that is how Benny came to fulfil his task. He looked again at Hope, but Hope seemed to have forgotten that he was there.

Benny turned to go, but then he thought of something just in time. 'Oh, I almost forgot! My mother, Candela, sends you her love.'

Hope chuckled. It was a happy sound. He raised a hand to accept the message. With one last look, Benny turned to leave.

'Wait for me!' bellowed Far, as she hopped a ride on Benny's nose. 'Come then,' chatted Far in a voice filled with hope, 'let's go and find the rest of your friends.'

Hoot had left the garden and was flying inside the tower when suddenly he saw the snails far below. *Well, well,* he thought, *are they looking, dare I say it, almost like friends?* He smiled to himself. *Bibs and Bobs friends? No more bickering and competing for attention?*

'Bobs, Bibs, hail to you,' he called, as he swept in a merry dance up and down the great hall.

'Oh Hoot,' cried Bobs, 'we were so lost! Thank goodness you're here.'

'There's no time to lose, my friends. We must find

Benny,' Hoot replied. 'Let's hurry!'

The three rushed off. As they went, Hoot and Bibs told each other all that had happened. Even Bobs was caught up in the talk as he gravely told them his part of the story. But no matter how weird, scary, or good, the best part of all was to be together again.

'The sooner Hope is found and we can all leave this place, the happier I'll be, that's for sure,' whispered Bibs.

'Yes,' Hoot nodded, 'Benny was right. This place is not for the likes of us.'

They knew that Benny might still need their help to find Hope so they hurried together, up the long hallways of the tower. On and on they went, until like a blessing, they heard the clip and clop of hooves. They dashed toward the sound and, sure enough, they came face to face with Benny. Oddly, a butterfly sat on his nose.

'Ahuh!' grinned the butterfly. 'Didn't I tell you that we'd find them here?'

Much ado of greeting and laughter followed as the four friends reunited.

'I found Bibs!' called an elated Bobs.

Benny chuckled at this odd turn of events.

'I found them both!' laughed Hoot.

Benny's eyes sparkled. 'I knew Hoot would find you,' he said with a grin, 'and I also have news. I found Hope!'

A sigh of relief went up from the others. No matter how hard this journey had been, at least now it all had some meaning.

In a gush of storytelling, Bibs told of his wild sprint. Bobs quietly told of his run-in with Hate, and how he couldn't believe his eyes when he found Bibs asleep. He blustered a bit when he told that part.

Benny smiled at Hoot and Hoot knew what he was thinking; the two Imperial Guard snails had re-written history!

'It was such a relief,' beamed Hoot, 'when I found these two, bedraggled but safe. I must say though, Benny, that your news from Hope is the best news of all.'

'I knew you could do it, Benny,' called Bibs.

'I knew, before you knew, that he could do it,' cried Bobs.

For a moment, everyone held their breath. Was this friendship going to be short lived? Soon, though, Bobs began to chuckle, then Bibs joined in. Relieved, so did Benny and Hoot. Far rolled her eyes and the others laughed more.

'Well then,' Benny began after a while, 'we've done what we came for, so now we go home.'

'Ahem,' grunted Far, 'may I introduce myself, please?'

Immediately, Benny realised that with all the talk and telling of tales, he'd forgotten to introduce Hope's butterfly. However, before Benny could speak, Far carried on.

'You must be Bobs,' she began. 'How selfless and thoughtful you are for saving Bibs on your own.' Bobs, who was normally so dour and sour, blushed bright pink. Pretty girls never spoke much to him.

Far turned to Bibs. 'You must be Bibs. Benny told me how brave you can be.' Bibs shuffled and pretended to be shy.

'Ah, Hoot,' Far smiled, 'I know you're Benny's right

hand man and I also know that you are wise and kind.'
Hoot bowed low.

Then, done with her introductions, and pleased they'd
gone well, Far perched back onto Benny's nose.

'It's time, everyone,' Benny urged. 'Time to go home
to our own world.' The travellers turned for the door.
They reached it quickly enough. Benny didn't hesitate.
'Come on,' he insisted, 'let's go home.' They were almost
over the bridge when Benny stopped.

'What is it?' Hoot frowned.

Benny peered at the owl. Pain flashed through his brow.

'We have trouble, Hoot,' he whispered. 'My headache
has returned.'

Even as he said the words, the Sorcerer of Great
Contempt appeared darkly before them, blocking the
end of the bridge. He was no longer the frail old man that
Rielle had met. His livid eyes pinned them from under
dark brows as he stood strong and tall.

'So,' he rasped, 'you thought you had won,' he spat at
Benny. 'You thought you had escaped. You thought you
had it all worked out, didn't you, unicorn? Now you will
see that there's no escape from me!'

Benny sighed. He was tired of Wish. He wanted to go
home. It had been a long journey to the Tower of Dreams
and he missed the forest and the wholesome herd.

So much had happened to the travelling four. They had
begun this journey with faith in their hearts, leaving the
safe forest and their beloved homes. They had travelled
to these shores and to this strange land, fought a battle
and made some wonderful friends, but they'd also been

lost and painfully burned. It was impossible not to be changed by that!

Benny sent a thought to Candela and Coraggio. Immediately, he saw them in his mind's eye. With the vision of them, his heart surged with the Ritual of Return. Benny tossed his head and arched his neck as he oozed power sent from the herd.

The Sorcerer of Great Contempt was surprised, but amused. The unicorn was defying him! He wasn't sure whether he should laugh or capture him where he stood. It was the moment of pause that Benny needed.

'Come on!' Benny called to the others. Turning, he dove into the moat and began to swim.

Bibs and Bobs bolted past the sorcerer as he stood open-mouthed.

Hoot escaped on a current of wind, and Far, who was new to this cut and run, just managed to grab Bibs' antenna and hold on tightly.

Benny powered through the water as it whooshed around him. Reaching what he felt was a safe distance he climbed onto land and hurriedly looked back.

The sorcerer was frozen to the spot, half way through throwing a ball of fire! Behind him, as sweetly as the breeze of a mild spring day, there piped the faun. While he fluted, the grass around the sorcerer grew and grew, and as it did so, swift, strong tendrils reached up from the ground and pulled him down.

Hoot joined Benny and the snails. They listened as the music held the sorcerer to the ground and they watched as he howled, disappearing from sight.

With joy and delight the faun played on, and even from the hill where they were standing, the travellers could see the almond trees sway. Around the sorcerer the grass grew taller as trees spouted growth and birds chirped louder. Even the moat began to play, as small white waves swished with the game.

The sorcerer was gone. He seemed to have sunk and been consumed.

'Ah,' smiled Bibs, 'I've wanted to know who the little faun was, and, well, now I think I understand.'

So once more they turned for home, and this time the bedraggled friends finally arrived at the sandy shores.

'Half an hour late,' called a voice. There, with a flourish of friendliness, was a smiling Oobaat. 'But that's not too bad considering what you've been through! Ah,' he continued, not at all surprised, 'a little butterfly. You would be Far, I presume?' And he bowed.

With great joy, the travellers greeted their old friend.

'All right,' Oobaat stated, 'you know the drill. I'll give you a ride!'

But before they went, Benny thought to ask, 'How did you know to wait for us, Oobaat?'

The tortoise beamed. 'Well, I've had some business of my own to attend to,' he chuckled, 'and let's just say, that I had a feeling you'd be finished here before long.' Then the tortoise looked long and hard at Benny. 'So tell me, young Benny, what did you think of the Tower of Dreams?'

'To be honest with you,' Benny soberly answered, 'it was nothing at all like I thought it would be.'

Oobaat just nodded with a knowing look.

So the travellers arranged themselves on Oobaat's large back and prepared themselves for the journey through the void.

Hoot whispered to tiny Far, who looked at a loss for what to do. 'Come, little one, you'd best not get wet. Hide under my wing where you'll be safe and stay dry.'

With everyone balanced and prepared, mighty Oobaat plunged deep into the water. Once again, the snails shut their eyes tightly, and Hoot balanced neatly on Benny's rump. A sense of relief was felt all round. They had accomplished their mission, with good news from Hope!

The first thing they heard as they surfaced through the wishing pond was Rana croaking with riotous joy.

'I did it! I did it!' he called, beaming smiles.

The tortoise turned one last time to Benny, Hoot, Bibs and Bobs. It was time to say goodbye to the valiant crew.

'You've done very well, Benemerito,' he praised. 'You've made your first journey a great success. Remember, little unicorn, that if you want, you can make your adventures become your friends.' With a fond smile he gave another big wink from his kind, wise eye, then bowed, and dove away.

Benny was thoughtful for a passing moment. He would miss the new friends who'd helped on this journey. He hoped he might meet them all again one day. The fading moonbeams surrounding the pond beckoned to him, eager to show him the road to go home.

'It's still the same night,' Benny murmured bemused as he looked around. 'What seemed like forever was just a matter of hours.'

'Ahh,' crooned Hoot, 'yes, young Benny, it certainly is the same night on which we departed. Who would have thought it, after all we've been through?'

'At last, back where we belong,' sighed Bobs, reluctant to show how old and tired he was.

'I need food, and lots of it,' chirped Bibs.

'Let me out!' squeaked Far.

Grinning, Hoot gently lifted his wing where a dry, safe Far flitted eagerly free. Shaking themselves and sending droplets flying, the others found that their coats, skins and shells were already drying.

So Benny, Hoot, Bibs and Bobs, and of course tiny Far, stepped onto the path to return to the forest. Barely able to be caught on the wind, the scent of almonds was fading away. Cool air brushed the travellers as night time took its cue, and stepped away to make room for a new day.

Rounding the tinkling brook, they arrived at the glade. There, where they had left them under the bank was a loudly snoring Pud and a soundly sleeping Rielle.

A gentle wicker broke through the air. The unicorns knew that Benny and his friends had returned.

With a wild buck of glee and an untamed gallop, Benny returned to the thick of the herd. Great joy was shown by all, and an enormous fuss was made!

Candela and Far met. Gently, the butterfly sat on Candela's brow, giving her news of Hope and the tower.

After the first greetings, Coraggio cleared his throat and stepped forward.

'Wise Hoot, stern Bobs and young brave Bibs, you've

all fully honoured your difficult tasks. We, the herd, Candela and I, cherish your bravery, your strength and your wits. Benny was well accompanied this night, and we are forever greatly in your debt.'

Coraggio bowed to the praiseworthy three. This was indeed a tribute coming from the mighty unicorn!

So for the snails and Hoot, it was over for now as they accepted and returned Coraggio's honourable bow. Then, saluting Benny, they left him with the herd.

Hoot flew off to his waiting family, where tales of the adventure would be repeated for days.

Bobs found a quiet, dark spot where he lay down to rest his old, weary bones.

Bibs zoomed off, impatient as usual. He wanted to eat and he wanted to sleep. There would be plenty of time later to think about all that had happened!

But just before the three disappeared, tiny Far blew each one a kiss.

As the sun made a gentle, new day's debut, the herd made music with the Ritual of Return. One by one they welcomed Benny, as the forest filled with enchantment and power.

CHAPTER 11

Truth will find me

Rielle awoke to the sound of gentle tunes. Smiling, she sat up. 'Dragon's fire... I've had a night of the most adventurous dreams!'

She remembered being lost, hungry and cold, and that an old tree had sheltered herself and Pud in a terrible storm. She looked around. This was another day. She and Pud were warm and snug under a mossy bank.

The music continued. Now she remembered... she had met Benny the unicorn! But wait: the storm had been two nights ago! She peered out from under the bank and saw unicorns greeting each other with musical joy. So the herd was real after all; that part was no dream.

'How lucky are we to be here, Pud?' she whispered with awe. 'They're real, Pud. This wasn't a dream. We're really in this forest with unicorns.'

Pud awoke and stretched every way he could, then he yawned, sneezed, licked Rielle's arm, and sat by her side.

Like a heart-wrenching shout, the sun greeted the morning, bursting through the forest with radiant warmth.

Rielle was overjoyed. She wasn't sure why, but she

felt better than she ever had. 'Oh, Pud,' she whispered, hugging him close, 'in my heart, I feel all new, somehow.' Tears of joy sat behind her eyes and a lump jumped in her throat.

Suddenly the forest stilled, as the chiming of horns ended in echoes.

Then Rielle remembered. 'Pud,' she breathed, with thick emotion, 'we went to Wish! I thought that was also just a dream, but it wasn't, was it? It really, truly happened. We went to Wish and I've just remembered how it all turned out!'

Pud placed a paw onto her foot then nudged her with his nose and looked curiously at her. *Of course they'd gone to Wish! How odd that something so important could have been remembered as a dream.*

'We went and we returned,' Rielle gasped. 'Pud, I've just remembered what happened there.'

Pud couldn't stand it any more. In the manner of all good dogs, he licked her once on the side of her face and nudged her so hard that she nearly fell over.

Rielle giggled, pushed him away and went on thoughtfully.

'We survived the storm, and then we came to this magical place, and… and, the unicorns put the star-scar on my brow. But, that wasn't enough for me, so I forced you to come through the perils of Wish.' She took Pud's face between her hands and looked him straight in the eyes.

'We survived it all, Pud, and, oh, I couldn't have made it without your help.' Rielle shivered. 'Can you forgive me for being so stubborn? Can you forgive me for the danger I put you through?'

Pud nudged her even harder, sending her backwards to land rather hard. But Rielle didn't notice. Her thoughts were in another place.

'That's right... we went to the Tower of Dreams and saw all those statues that looked as if they were ready to move! Then, urgh, that creepy old man, and the snake, Pud, the snake or tortoise or whatever he was.'

It wasn't my idea to go, thought Pud, but he listened attentively like a good dog.

'In some strange way,' continued Rielle, 'I think that snake, despite everything, was a really good friend. I mean, if it wasn't for him, we may never have returned.'

Then an idea struck her. 'Do you think that was the Ritual of Return we just heard, Pud?' Rielle looked around as excitement filled her voice. 'I wonder if it was in honour of Benny? If so, that means that he's also returned.'

Almost as if he heard her, Benny arrived at their little den. Politely, in case they were still asleep, he peered inside and saw that they were awake.

'Good morning, Rielle,' he beamed. 'How was your night? Did you sleep well?'

Rielle thought he looked different somehow, but then he gave her a huge cheeky grin, and Rielle knew that he hadn't changed.

'Thank you,' she smiled. 'I feel well this morning. In fact, I woke up feeling better than I have for ages.'

'I have to tell you something,' Benny said, becoming serious. 'Last night, while you slept, it was the right time to go, so Hoot, Bibs, Bobs and I went to Wish, and found the Tower of Dreams.'

Rielle marvelled at how it had been only one night!

'Oh!' she exclaimed, but found that she couldn't pretend, so she took a deep breath even as she hung her head. 'After you left, I snuck out of the forest, although Candela told me to stay.' She faltered, and then went on. 'I also went to Wish!' She glanced up and then looked away; she wouldn't bear it if she saw disappointment in Benny's eyes.

'Go on,' Benny urged, 'what did you find?'

'I... well, I didn't find Hope,' Rielle stammered, 'but I don't think I tried very hard.' As usual, Benny was listening to every word.

'You see,' Rielle continued, 'I don't know if I even realised it then, but I think I went to Wish for all the wrong reasons.'

She looked up, determined to face the truth of Benny's annoyance but Benny's expression was clear with no judgement in his eyes.

'I... I went to the tower, and there was no one there - just hundreds and hundreds of frozen statues. They were so lifelike, Benny, as if... as if they were waiting for me to tell them to move. I thought I might find you then, but I didn't. I panicked, and then I ran!'

'I ran outside into the garden. I thought that I'd been lucky and that I'd found Hope, but instead,' she shuddered, 'instead, I met a dreadful old man who seemed to know who you were. He wanted to take me prisoner and hurt faithful Pud. Oh Benny, that's when

Pud saved me, and we ran again, but I finally learned the meaning of the star-scar that's on my brow!'

'We got terribly lost and met an odd creature that could change shape. It was he who made me confront the truth, and he also helped us to come safely home.' Rielle faltered from her rush of words.

'I'm so sorry, Benny. I'm afraid my real reasons for going to Wish weren't... weren't truly honest or particularly good. I'm ashamed, and even worse, I don't seem to have achieved anything at all!'

As difficult as it was, she looked Benny squarely in the eyes. 'Please, please don't judge me, or think I'm bad.'

Benny tossed his marvellous head. 'Silly girl,' he smiled, 'haven't you learned anything yet? Unicorns don't waste time on judgement or regrets.'

Then Benny became serious, for he had his news to tell.

'Well then,' he continued in a grave tone, 'I have a message for you Rielle. I have to tell you that the message is from Hope.'

Rielle's heart jumped. She swallowed and felt sick. She was afraid to know what Hope had said. She and Benny stared tellingly at each other, and Rielle saw things in his eyes that she had never seen there before. She took a deep breath and hugged Pud tightly. The moment of reckoning was here with her now.

Did she still have a dream? Did Hope have an answer? Was there something for her out there? Would her heart ever mend?

She knew she could never have found Hope on her own. She had been too lost and too preoccupied to have known what to find. Dear, selfless Benny had succeeded, instead. Rielle didn't dare ask, and Benny was in no hurry, so she waited while Benny sat down on the grass.

'First, though,' he said, with a twinkle in his eye, 'I think you should hear about the adventures I've had.'

Then Benny told the tale of his brave ordeal and made much of the roles played by Hoot, Bibs and Bobs.

Rielle listened with laughter, and with fear, to the heart-stopping story that she heard. More often than not, she couldn't believe her ears. Had the travellers done all that for her? She knew she was the luckiest girl ever to be!

Benny paused, just after telling her how he'd found Hope.

This, then, was the moment that it was all about.

'Well,' he finally said as his green eyes sparkled, 'you needn't look so worried, for the news is good.'

Rielle held her breath and Pud sat up with his head to one side.

Benny beamed. 'Hope told me that you still have a dream!'

Rielle looked deeply into Benny's eyes. It was strange how she expected to feel different somehow. Inside her, though, it seemed that nothing had changed. She was still short of conviction and still unsure.

'Where, Benny? Where is my dream?' she whispered. 'My heart still feels lonely, and I'm still so unsure.'

'Look at me, Rielle,' Benny pleaded. 'Look more deeply into my eyes, and then tell me what you see.'

Rielle became nervous. She wished that Benny wouldn't confront her with these things. Confused and anxious, she quashed a familiar feeling of annoyance.

'I'm not sure what I'm looking for. I don't think I see

anything!' She gulped. She had imagined this moment very differently. 'I'm scared, Benny. I... I'm afraid to try. How do I dare trust that Hope is right?'

What if her heart never healed? What if she stayed sad forever?

'Look again, Rielle,' Benny insisted, 'but do something different. Don't look with your eyes; just see with your heart.'

She knew she had to try; she owed Benny that. He had her trust and her loyalty. After all, look what he had done and been through for her!

With fear and foreboding, Rielle opened her heart, where with timid baby steps, it tiptoed to truth. Suddenly the light shifted and the sun shone just so, and a glimmer of hope began to filter through.

Benny helped. 'Do you remember the first time we met, when Pud and I talked in the little glen? Do you remember how long it took for you to see me? It was Pud who saw me straight away, but tell me, Rielle, why do you think that was so?'

Again, Rielle remembered how it had been. Pud had seen Benny when she hadn't seen anything and had battled to understand. It seemed like ages ago now, but it had only been on the morning after the storm. Like a tiny tremble, thoughts trickled through her mind.

Who was Benny, really? Why was he so kind and so brave, just for her?

'You.... ' she began.

'Yes?' urged Benny.

In a rush of breath, Rielle finally answered.

'Well, I know you are brave. I know I can trust you

and that you're truly good and kind.' She stumbled for a thought and then went on. 'I, I think you love everything and everyone with a purity and honesty that is unusual and rare.'

Benny grinned. 'Yes! Pud saw me first, because animals feel love; they don't stop to question.' He pinned Rielle with happy, green eyes, as if content with a job well done. 'We unicorns are pure love... just as it was first invented, before love became a... well, an overused word. We are truth, kindness and honour, the courage to do what is right, friendship without betrayal, good deeds and sacrifice. Actions are stronger than words, Rielle!'

Rielle gasped at the squeeze of her heart. As if sensing a hint of doubt, Benny nodded at her, and in that blinding moment, Rielle understood what her heart had always known.

'The riddle of unicorns!' Rielle exclaimed, as silver shivers ran down her spine.

'Yes,' breathed Benny. He looked earnestly at her, willing her to remember the words he would say next.

'When you question your wandering ways, and when it seems that you have no home. When the darkness of night stays through the day, and you feel there is no one who understands. When you see yourself as unloved, unwanted and alone, then whisper this riddle and know it to be true.'

Truth will find me
I have no fear
I have found the unicorn.

Benny's eyes sparkled. 'I want you to remember those words, Rielle.' He paused and then in his most sincere voice, he went on. 'When you have your saddest moments, or even when your heart breathes joy, no matter what happens, or how things look, you are always loved, just for who you are.'

Then Benny became quiet and his green eyes half-closed as if he had accomplished a great effort of work.

'You see, Rielle, you had to know who I was, and you had to understand, before I could give you your gift from Hope.'

As if on cue, Far fluttered forward and flew straight to Rielle.

'Oh,' smiled Rielle with swift delight, 'a butterfly!'

Benny became formal again.

'Rielle, this little butterfly is your gift from Hope, to keep your heart happy, bright and alert. To remind you that your dreams are alive, and that your fears will pass. Just so that you know that even in your darkest hours, there is someone in your corner for you, so you may still find strength. And the greatest truths that your heart needs to know are that you are precious and unique, and that you must love yourself first.' With a bow, Benny whispered, 'I now lend you Far, Hope's butterfly.'

Far flew with purpose to Rielle before settling on her shoulder.

Rielle felt fat tears on her cheeks. Dearest little Benny, the unicorn friend she was blessed to have made! True to his words he was all of those things, and he'd proved that Hope existed to her with his unselfish deeds. She opened her mouth through her happy tears to thank him, and to tell him how he'd changed her life.

But Benny jumped up, and looking Rielle full in the face, he planted a quick cheerful kiss right on her forehead. He laughed then - the happiest laugh - and bucked and galloped joyfully away through the glade.

Rielle couldn't help giggling. His joy was infectious and so was his mirth, and on her shoulder, Far chuckled as well.

Rielle put her hand up to wipe the tears from her eyes, but when she looked again, Benny was gone.

'Benny?' she queried.

Pud began to howl.

'Benny?' Rielle got up and ran through the glade, but as hard as she and Pud searched, it seemed that Benny was gone.

'Benny!' she called again.

Pud howled, and his eyes followed movement or invisible shadows.

Like the wind roaring a gale, the sound of the herd's hooves galloping, filled the forest. Leaves swished and grass swayed, as Pud and Rielle trembled with the power. Then, before they knew it, the forest was still.

Once more in the distance, like a fond farewell, they heard the echo and trilling of a unicorn call. As if through a dream, the world became hushed, and for long moments all was silent and nothing moved.

'They've gone, Pud,' Rielle whispered. 'Shall we ever see them again, I wonder, our special unicorn friends?'

Pud stared into the forest with a furrowed, sad brow.

'Funny how something so short-lived was so perfect.' Rielle choked on her words. 'And how what I fought against will now be so missed. I thought for some reason that this wonder and magic would always be there, and yet, just two days ago, I didn't know it existed at all.'

She looked down at Pud and he looked up, and his amber eyes reflected how much they'd both changed.

Rielle sighed. On warm, windless nights, she knew that she would listen with longing for the sweet, sad call of unicorns.

'Don't worry, Pud,' she murmured, patting his head, 'Benny's still with us in our thoughts and our hearts. For now, though, well, we have to keep walking, for we probably have a long way to go. I... I've got a dream... a dream to find!'

Far had sat quietly, then, in a butterfly whisper she flew onto Rielle's nose.

Rielle laughed. 'I hope you aren't going to sit on my nose the whole way?'

'No,' Far replied, 'not if it keeps making you go all cross-eyed, but I have to tell you, Rielle, that it seems that your journey has just begun. It might take a while to find your dream. I hope you know what I mean.'

Rielle sighed. She knew that she had changed a great deal because she wasn't annoyed. 'Yes, well,' she replied, with a wistful smile, 'this is real life, isn't it? Journeys only end in fairy tales.'

The Dream's Beginning

Shadows were burying the day as the sun retreated in gracious defeat.

'That's the end of the story, dear children.' The traveller stopped speaking.

'Ooohh,' we moaned. We wanted to hear more! We wanted perfect endings so that all the answers could be ours.

I was sad. Surely, the tale wasn't over already. I looked at the others. In the long, darkened shadows of dusk, their eyes reflected what I felt.

'What happened,' we asked, 'after they galloped away?'

The traveller looked thoughtfully at us.

'Well,' she hesitated, before going on, 'Rielle kept her word. She travelled far and wide in search of her dream, but before you ask, well, that's a whole other story for another day. As time went by, the mark made by unicorns remained on her brow and she let it guide her to avoid danger. It never let her down.' She smiled a big wide smile for the very first time then began to get up, but we wanted to know more.

'And, the herd?' I begged.

'I can tell you only this,' she murmured, 'and it's the best thing of all.'

We cheered. 'Tell us, tell us,' we called, our voices shrill with need. 'What is the best thing? What? What?'

In a whisper, as if she were sharing the greatest secret ever told, the traveller leaned forward, her eyes sparkling brightly despite the dullness of evening.

'When the sun shifts and shines in a special way,' she announced, 'and the forest is lit just so, watch carefully for a flash of white and then listen, and you will hear the gallop of hooves. On clear nights when the moon is hunting, take note and you will hear echoes of a call. You will know, then, that if the path is broken or there is danger ahead, not far away, and somewhere before you, are Benny and the unicorn herd.'

She stopped, then drew back from us and grasped her walking staff.

'Will we ever see Benny out there in the forest? Will we? Will we, do you think?' we pleaded.

But it was over. This time, even our need and wide-eyed faces failed to draw the response that we wanted.

'I think I hear your parents calling,' she said.

Indeed, our parents were beckoning and reluctantly, we stood to leave.

The traveller smiled and said one last thing. 'You can pat the dog if you like. I'm sure he'd think that was nice.'

With smiles and hugs we made much of the beast, as he whined quietly, grinned, and wagged his old tail.

'Thank you!' we called, as we turned to go.

Then we ran to our dinners and our warm homes and

hearths, as children should always do, but our heads were still brimming with courage, Hope, the mystery of truth, and unicorns.

I reached a grove of trees and stopped, for I just had to give one last wave. I looked back to the bench where we'd all been gathered, but the traveller and her dog were gone.

A last shaft of sunlight burst generously through the trees and helped patterns dance on the twilit ground. The breeze rustled leaves as it stepped through trees, and there, dancing with joy, in silence and alone, was a tiny bright blue butterfly.

The Unicorns of Wish Books

WISH

WISH AGAIN

THE THIRD WISH

HOPE

JOURNEY OF TREES

About the Author

Deby Adair is a writer and artist. She loves all animals and believes we must take care of our natural world.

UnicornKisses

www.ingramcontent.com/pod-product-compliance
Lightning Source LLC
Chambersburg PA
CBHW030647110726
47901CB00002B/602